A Pearl Before Spies

More from Phase Publishing
by
Rebecca Connolly

Agents of the Convent
Fortune Favors the Sparrow

The Ears Have It

Of Mist and Mirrors

A Trick of Fate

The Arrangements
An Arrangement of Sorts

Married to the Marquess

Secrets of a Spinster

The London League
The Lady and the Gent

A Rogue About Town

A Tip of the Cap

The Spinster Chronicles
The Merry Lives of Spinsters

The Spinster and I

Spinster and Spice

Agents of the Convent
Book Five

Rebecca Connolly

Phase Publishing, LLC
Seattle

Phase Publishing, LLC first paperback edition
March 2025

ISBN 978-1-952103-75-9
Library of Congress Control Number 2025902030
Cataloging-in-Publication Data on file.

Acknowledgements

To Jane Eyre, the most underrated heroine fiction has ever produced. Poor, obscure, plain, and little she may be… but oh, heavens, she is fierce. This one's for the Janes in the world.

And to Liquid IV. Thanks for keeping me conscious and vertical.

Want to hear about future releases and upcoming events for Rebecca Connolly?

Sign up for the monthly Wit and Whimsy at:

www.rebeccaconnolly.com

A Proclamation

By Miss Leonora Masters
Headmistress of Miss Masters's Finishing School

Forasmuch as it has been thus Ordained by the powers that be that the Rearing of gently bred ladies requires some assistance, and in Keeping with traditions long established, It has been decreed that such rearing Needs proper establishment for training purposes, Given the span and scope of such development.

As it pleases the powers that be, Never forgetting the honor due to her subjects, Development and education of young ladies shall be Courteously and courageously given.

Owing to the need for such establishment, Unto the finishing of the female sex, Nobility shall be thus encouraged, Their patronage much desired, to Relinquish the education of such female persons as aforementioned Yet in their youthful and less informed state Into such qualified care.

Nevertheless, with charity and succor, females of a Lesser status shall be generously and Indubitably sponsored in their similar attendance herein For the purpose of gaining appropriate Education as befits needs and station.

Occupied thusly, this establishment shall henceforth Render such superior instruction and care, Defending the virtue and honor of her pupils, Engendering appropriate accomplishment upon all, Avowing to maintain the standards and Traditions of her forebears, and shall Henceforth fulfil all other obligations as so indicated.

Given under my Hand at Miss Masters's Finishing School in Kent, the 1ˢᵗ day of March, 1790, in the Thirtieth year of His Majesty's reign.

God save the King
Leonora Masters

Chapter One
Guernsey, 1827

$\mathcal{A}$bigail Charteris had never been more pleased to have her feet on solid ground.

Ever.

Years upon years of training in the realms of covert operations, and still she had not managed to build up an immunity to seasickness. She'd spent ages of time on the European continent in her younger years for various missions, and she had been unwell on the voyages, but she could not remember it being so debilitating back then.

Granted, she had been younger, stronger, and less aware of her precious mortality at the time, but even so.

Her head was still swimming while she stepped down from the dock at which her ship had landed, looking about her for the porter managing luggage. Taking slow breaths in through her nose and out of her mouth seemed to be keeping her nausea from overpowering her, and once she had her belongings, she could find some quiet place to sit and recover before heading on to her final destination. She was not expected until the evening, and it was barely midday.

Plenty of time.

The air of Guernsey was delightfully fresh and sprinkled with an air of jasmine, at least to Abby's senses. It reminded her of when she had first come to the Miss Masters's School for Fine Young Ladies in Kent and had taken a trip to the coastline itself. She never noticed the change in air texture or fragrance anymore, as it had become her home and her usual state, but she had never been to Guernsey before. She hadn't anticipated feeling so refreshed so early in her trip.

She hadn't anticipated anything about Guernsey at all. She was too focused on her assignment and her role here. Guernsey itself had been irrelevant.

But from what she could see and tell at the moment, she had high hopes that any unoccupied time of hers might be spent enjoying the particular beauty and refreshment this place had to offer.

She had no promise of unoccupied time, of course, and her handicapped leg prevented any real exploration or adventure, unless she wished to be confined to a chair or divan for up to a week in recovery. Her weakness and limp did not prevent her from much, as far as the average life activities went, but it did put a damper on exploration. And riding. And speed. And…

Well, anything that would make her the operative she had once been.

Which was why this opportunity was so crucial to her. It was the first time in five years that she would be able to take on an assignment that was not based at the school, instructing future operatives. This time, she *was* an operative, albeit a rather peculiar one.

She even had a new code name.

Pearl.

It felt strange to take that on, rather like a new taste in her mouth she was not yet certain of. A new name was a new persona, and she did not feel at all like a precious gem. She'd enjoyed her time as Sage very much in the years of her almost frantic activity. She had been wholly devoted to whatever assignment or cause she'd been asked to take up, and risked everything for it, be it heart, body, or soul.

Until one day, her mission had actually taken her body. Or rather, her escape from danger had broken and twisted her leg so badly that her life would never be the same.

One ought not to recklessly ride a horse while injured if it could be helped at all. Being thrown from such creatures under those circumstances could prove disastrous.

It had taken Abby a full year to even manage the ability to mount a horse again, let alone capably ride one. Even now, she could not do more than trot, but it was something.

A faint buzzing in her cheeks prompted her to sit on a nearby log for fear of swooning entirely. She stretched out her weak leg and patted it gently, more to hide her frustrations than anything else. No one passing on the docks seemed to pay her any mind, which was just how she preferred it.

There were advantages to being a plain woman of a certain age, make no mistake.

But, oh, she would give anything for a body that did not grow weary so quickly, a head that did not ache frequently, and a mind that did not work slowly.

She was being a little ridiculous. She was only three and thirty, after all. She was not decrepit.

She was just not accustomed to an active sort of life anymore.

It was only a few moments before she felt more to rights and pushed to her feet, moving along the docks once more with the others who had come off the ship. There weren't many who seemed to be here for pleasure, but then, neither was she.

She was here in Guernsey to work.

Miss Abigail Chorley, governess.

It ought to be simple enough, as she was a teacher already. Her pupils here would be much younger than her usual students, but that could be as refreshing as the change in location.

She had dealt with tyrannical girls in their adolescence. How difficult could two actual children be?

Abby snorted softly to herself as she began scanning the docks for her trunks. She had been a tyrannical child, along with her two brothers. It would serve her right to have to teach rambunctious little ones with such advance judgments.

She caught sight of her trunk, most notable for the scratch along one face that resembled a scripted letter C made by a particularly unwieldy hand. Her income from the school was adequate, but hardly enough to spend recklessly, and there seemed little point in procuring a new trunk when she never went anywhere. So the damage from her last venture—her recuperation and recovery at a very secret residence in Norfolk—had been allowed to remain as a memento of the life she had been forced to leave behind.

Now she winced at seeing it. What would her employer think if such a sign of damage was seen?

Of course, this was only a temporary position of employment, but Abigail Chorley was not necessarily supposed to be a poor governess who could not afford a new trunk. And it seemed monstrously unjust that just because Abigail Charteris chose not to spend her money thus, the new governess should suffer so.

But it was much too late now.

Mr. Bichard would simply have to make his own judgments about Miss Chorley, should the blemish on her trunk be something he noticed.

She doubted he would. These powerful fathers of young children never paid attention to the details of the help, and her hiring for the position of governess had been overseen by the housekeeper anyway. Mrs. Corbin had seemed particularly pleased by Abby's application and references, and their correspondence had been nothing but cordial and warm. She knew Abby was a woman of employment, as any governess they hired would be, and could not expect her to have the best luggage.

Women of similar station understood these things.

Abby made her way to her trunk, heaving it away from the others with a nod to the porter. It was hardly a ladylike thing to do, but she was no lady here. In fact, she was a nobody. And as a nobody, there would not be any special accommodations made for her arrival. Besides, she had only informed the house that she would be arriving today, not when.

"Miss Chorley?"

She jerked to a halt, eyes widening as she looked around. No one here should know her name yet, fictional or otherwise. Could she possibly be compromised already? Or was this another one of those impossible coincidences like what had happened when Mist and Mirrors had used the same lapsed title last year?

Still, she would continue to act as normally as possible. She had no other options.

"Yes?" she replied to the open air, unsure who was calling her.

A kind-faced man in farmer's clothing approached, sweeping the flat cap from his head. "Begging your pardon, Miss Chorley. My name is Simms. I am the gamekeeper at Coutanche House. Mrs. Corbin asked if I would look out for you today, as your ship was coming in. May I take your trunk?"

Abby smiled with precious, unexpected relief. "Please," she replied gratefully. "I am a touch ungainly with it."

Simms flashed a quick grin and took the trunk from her. "Most men are ungainly with a trunk, Miss Chorley. You managed well enough."

"Well, I do have a limp, so it complicates matters." She gestured to her weak leg without dramatics.

"I noticed," Simms said without affectation, giving her a firm nod. "And as I said, you managed well enough." He gestured in the direction of a plain but sturdy wagon parked nearby. "It is not a far drive, but we should leave quickly. The winds are so changeable here, and the roads grow almost impassable for a wagon if it rains."

Bemused, Abby tilted her head as Simms hoisted her trunk into the bed of the wagon. "And here I was informed the island has more predictable weather than England."

Simms barked a rough laugh. "We do, miss. It is only the wind that plagues us, and I still find it better than Cornish winds." He came over and offered her a hand into the wagon seat.

"Are you Cornish, Simms?" she asked as she sat, adjusting her coat and skirts.

"Once I was, yes. Now I consider this my home." He nodded again and came around to the driver's seat, flicking the reins as soon as he was seated.

A few moments after they were away from the port, it became evident that Simms was not a particularly loquacious individual. Abby didn't mind this. In fact, it rather gave her the opportunity to observe her surroundings without appearing distant to anyone.

Guernsey was not a large island, that much she knew. In the weeks leading up to her arrival, she had learned everything possible about its history, its culture, its people, its geography… It was, in fact, entirely possible to walk the entire island's perimeter in a day.

Not for Abby, of course, but for an able-bodied person with the stamina to do so.

Entirely possible and not altogether illogical.

Quaint. That was the word she had been searching for. Guernsey seemed especially quaint, and she would have said so if there were a way to express it without sounding completely patronizing. She had no intention of making enemies of the locals by giving the impression of demeaning their home, so she would hold her tongue until she managed to say something safer and just as apt. But there was no escaping the fact that the island was small. It was also more French than English, historically and geographically, but had been considered English for long enough that it was not even a question.

Which meant it could be a lovely little seat of treason, for all intents and purposes. The Faction could have a strong and steady heartbeat in a place like this.

Where she saw quaintness and charm, they might see opportunity and convenience. Where she saw beauty and refreshment, they might see an outpost and ripe fields. Where she saw a small island of rich heritage, they might see potential for recruitment.

She would need to watch every step she took, not just her steps in Coutanche House.

Calm yourself, Abs, she silently scolded with as much harshness as she dared. Barely half an hour on the island, and already she was imagining some massive coup among the entire population.

The sooner she started living her new life as Abigail Chorley, the better.

"Don't say much, Miss Chorley," Simms grunted beside her, his hands perfectly steady.

Smiling, Abby glanced at him. "Neither do you. I am happy to make conversation if you like, but silence does not perturb me."

Again, Simms grunted. "That'll serve you well at Coutanche."

"Oh? Am I to expect silence? I thought the girls were rather small, so I anticipated… well, noise, I suppose." Abby shrugged, not at all ashamed of her presumption and hoping Simms might give her some idea of what to expect before they arrived.

She watched as the lines formed and reformed around Simms's mouth, his stubble doing nothing to hide them. "The girls are bright little things, I'll grant you that. Sunshine under the right circumstances, though I haven't seen them as such in a long while. The house is very quiet most of the time, and that'll be due to Mr. Bichard. Moody sort, but not harsh or cruel. Very brooding, and the daughters feed off that, in my view. I know Mrs. Corbin feels the same, but none of us will ever say so."

"No, I imagine not," Abby murmured, tucking a strand of unruly hair behind her ear. "Has it always been like that?"

Simms shook his head. "Only since Mrs. Bichard died. A year and a half ago, almost. All the sunshine went out of the house when she did. The master lost all his heart there. I think he visits the girls regular enough, but there is no playing. Mind, he was not that playful before. Serious sort. Not a bad thing, of course, just the way he is. Only the mistress ever broke him free of it."

Strange how talkative Simms had become with only the slightest urging. But Abby had developed the ability to read people with decent accuracy in her career, and she could see and feel that he was fond of the family he worked for. It was an encouraging sign but could also significantly hinder Abby's assignment.

The man whose children she would be tending, Gilles Bichard, was a member of a secret faction of French citizens, supporters, and covert operatives trying to overthrow their present British government and implement a version of Napoleon's schemes that Sieyès had envisioned in the early days of the Revolution.

Not only was he a member of the Faction, but Bichard had been part of a plot to abduct a young woman from London so he could marry her and gain access to London Society to further the Faction's aims.

Well, he had not actually taken part in the abduction, but he was the prospective bridegroom for the woman who had been abducted.

And now Abby was tasked with investigating him under the guise of being governess to his young daughters.

She needed to be trusted by everyone associated with the family, and she also needed to be ready to destroy the perfect little life of lies Bichard had set up for himself.

But not right away, and not until she was sure. And not until she had received orders to do so. It was entirely possible that he would be left alone for now and watched until the time was right to intervene.

If it ever was.

Abby ground her teeth together as they bumped along in the wagon. She would love to upend Bichard's life herself, should she discover he had direct involvement with what had happened at Christmas. One of her fellow teachers at the Miss Masters's School had been the one abducted, and Abby was particularly fond of Lucy Allred. The abduction had been foiled—twice—and Lucy was now married to Hunter Mortimer, who was a bit of an enigma, but wholly devoted to her. She was still teaching at the school this term, as Mrs. Mortimer, and though not one of the operatives herself, was now fully involved in the true mission of the school and students.

Training female covert operatives for England.

Abby had a sneaking suspicion that Hunter Mortimer was actually the operative known as Trick, but such things were almost never confirmed unless strictly necessary. Still, she had privately assured Lucy that she would find out the truth and do her very best work in preventing anyone else from the fate that Lucy had nearly been subjected to.

Infiltration was not something that Abby had taken part in for some time, but she was rather good at keeping her traditional finishing-school pupils from understanding other aims and corners of the school, as well as some of the other teachers.

She prayed that would be practice enough. Her quick and improvised refreshment training had not been particularly promising, but when nothing physical could be required, what else could she do?

"Do you think," Abby ventured in a hesitant voice, "that Mr. Bichard would object to a little less silence around the house? I should like to let the girls be enthusiastic and childlike in all respects. There is nothing so unnerving as a perfectly silent child."

"I could not agree more, Miss Chorley," Simms echoed with a firm nod. "I think that, once you are settled, you might broach the subject with the master. I know he loves his girls, so he just might see the idea in a fair light."

Abby could hear his own hesitation, no matter how he tried to hide it. "But he might not?"

Simms exhaled noisily. "But he might not. Only time will tell."

It was all Abby could do not to quirk a smile and a brow at the same time at the irony.

Indeed, yes.

Only time would tell.

Chapter Two

"The new governess has arrived, sir."

Gilles Bichard lifted his head from his hand and looked at the plump figure of the housekeeper in the doorway to his study. "Pardon?"

Mrs. Corbin looked a trifle perturbed, but not entirely surprised. "I said the selection of fish was not as fresh at the market so Cook has had to settle for cod. The gardens are beginning to bloom already, so Mr. Mangum will be bringing his help in earlier than normal—"

Gilles brushed his hand in front of his face, cutting her off. "No, no, I heard all of that. What was it you said at the end?"

Her trim brows rose just a touch, and Gilles had employed her long enough to know that she did not believe he heard anything she had said, be it the first or second time.

She was correct, of course, but he would not admit it.

"The new governess has arrived," Mrs. Corbin repeated in a too-clear tone, undoubtedly for his benefit. "Simms arrived with her from the port not long ago. She is getting settled in her rooms, and I will be meeting with her later. I just thought you would wish to know."

Gilles blinked once, then again. Yes, he would wish to know, but not the day the new governess was arriving. He would have wished to know weeks prior to this. What had happened to their previous governess? Madeline and Marie-Claire were only just old enough for lessons, and there was some debate, in his mind, whether Marie-Claire was actually old enough, but she would not enjoy being left out of something that Madeline was doing.

There was just over a year between the girls, and where it had been a trial at first, it was delightful and convenient now.

"Sir?"

Gilles blinked an awkward third time as he was brought back to the present moment.

Right. Governess.

"Did I know we were getting a new governess?" Gilles asked the housekeeper in what he hoped was an imperious tone.

"I informed you of the need, sir, when it was apparent."

Zut. Gilles forced his expression to remain blank. "And what became of our previous governess?"

Mrs. Corbin cleared her throat. "She ran off with the Pelley lad from St. Sampson. I have been seeking her replacement for three months."

Three months?

Gilles knew he was a trifle distracted with other matters in his life, as the constant rambling in his mind could attest, but three months? That was excessive, even for him.

"Ah, yes," he replied, very belatedly. "Now I recollect. If you don't mind, I think I shall meet her tomorrow. It is late, and there is no need for her to change her attire just for me. She can meet the girls in the morning, of course, and there is no need to hasten the start of her lessons. I shall leave it to the pair of you to decide when is best. *Les chéris* do best when on friendly terms, as you know."

"Yes, sir. I had anticipated tomorrow being something of an introduction for Miss Chorley, both to the house and to the girls. If the weather is fair, perhaps a walk. I shall let her ease into instruction as she sees fit." Mrs. Corbin lowered her chin just a touch, giving him a surveying look that reminded him of his several childhood nannies. "Will you be taking supper in here, sir?"

Gilles was not entirely certain if he was being scolded for something, if she was disappointed in him, if he had irked her in some way, or if she was simply anxious to be out of his sight, which made determining the appropriate reaction difficult.

And Mrs. Corbin had a way that made him feel like an unruly child most of the time anyway.

"Yes, please, Mrs. Corbin," he murmured in as respectful and subservient a tone as could be tolerated. "If it is not too much trouble."

Her expression became almost entirely pitying. "No trouble at all, sir. I will have it brought to you shortly."

Gilles nodded, smiling just a little. *"Merci."*

The door to his study closed with a soft click, and he sat back in his chair roughly, exhaling through sputtering lips.

That could have gone better in at least a dozen ways.

His life had not always been complicated enough to leave him in a constant state of distraction, but it was his way of life now. His tasks were not something he could speak about to anyone, which meant he had to turn everything over in his mind three or four times before taking any action. His daughters were young and still attached to him, so what little unoccupied time he did have ought to be devoted to them.

Ought to be.

Finding available energy for his daughters was growing more and more difficult.

He just did not have enough to give to each of his necessary avenues.

Not without Heloise.

His throat constricted almost painfully, and he shook his head rather hard, willing the images of his late wife from his mind. Eighteen months without her, and still he was lost. Not in the same ways he had been lost in those early days, weeks, and months, but lost all the same. The agony had faded with time, as he had been assured it would, and he had settled into the feeling of life without the woman he loved.

He did not enjoy it, but it had become normal.

He was not good at it, but it had become normal.

He was still in pain all the time, but it had become normal.

Heloise had been so many things to him. His wife, his lover, his vision, his guide, his partner… She had excelled at all of them, which should not have been a surprise, as he had fallen for her within moments of meeting her. Why should she not have been as majestic in reality as she had been in his perception? But what he had not anticipated was how that love for her would grow.

Rapidly, as it happened. Recklessly. Helplessly.

Consumingly.

And with that love had come their daughters in rapid succession.

As had his present position as a double agent in a very dangerous game.

He hadn't meant to be anything of the sort when he and his brother had joined the organization in France that wished to rid itself of the monarchy upon its return. The group that thought Napoleon had held a decent objective but had pursued it with reckless actions and had spent the last several years working to bring the more subtle maneuvering of such objectives about. They were both passionate Frenchmen, after all, and would do anything to see France rise to the heights it deserved.

Well, almost anything.

With every passing year, Gilles saw this devoted Faction to which he belonged sinking itself into deeper and darker depths than he was comfortable with. His brother knew nothing of his struggles, and still believed every word the Faction said, fully devoted to their cause. It had taken Gilles some time to admit his doubts, even to himself, and then when he did, he discovered that his wife, the woman he had fallen in love with, was actively working against the very Faction he had been so dedicated to.

The timing was fortunate, however. They'd had the most intimate and raw conversation of their entire relationship and come to the conclusion that they could do some extraordinary good in the world by working together, with Gilles remaining embedded in the Faction and Heloise strengthening her connections with England. Through those connections, Gilles had been able to develop a working friendship with an operative in England for himself, and he had been able to send crucial information to him from time to time via a mutual contact.

Then Heloise had taken ill and never recovered, leaving the weight of their entire subversive operation on his shoulders alone.

His mind was not as quick without her. He was even more certain than before that the Faction needed to be stopped, and if nothing else, he owed it to Heloise to see her vision fulfilled. But it had been something they had both worked towards for the years they'd had, and it felt far more intimidating a prospect by himself.

The only relief he had in any of this was that he lived on the island of Guernsey rather than in France itself. It would have been far more difficult to manage any of this if he had been in the heart of the Faction operations. He might have been a more informative asset for the British if he were, but the Faction found him particularly valuable living on British soil, so he was kept very well informed as it was.

Heloise had asked them to leave Brittany, where he grew up, and move to Guernsey for a quieter life, and he had been more than willing to do so. Now he was even more grateful for her foresight. Their daughters had a lovely and uncomplicated life in a country setting without being restricted in any way, and the beauty of an island upbringing was giving each of them a stronger sense of curiosity and appreciation for the world than they might have had otherwise.

But he would admit, Guernsey was too quiet for him with Heloise gone. His home was too quiet. His life was too quiet.

He was not a loud man, and Heloise had not been particularly boisterous either. Yet somehow, his life was drowning in silence and had been since her death.

Gilles had always wanted a quiet life. But not this quiet.

Rubbing at his brow, he pushed up from his desk and moved out of his study, finding nothing encouraging or stimulating in there. It seemed that, more and more, it was the room where his mind spun rather than any work got accomplished. Frustration upon frustration built upon him, and everything became frenetic and confusing.

If he did not find a way to live his complicated life with some orderliness soon, he would begin to fail in obvious ways rather than just private ones.

He made his way out of the house, knowing he would not have much time before Mrs. Corbin had that tray of supper brought to his study. But he was presently desperate for fresh air and that now-familiar feeling of Guernsey's winds whipping at his hair and clothing. He wouldn't go far; he rarely did anymore.

Hands clenching and unclenching, Gilles strode to the large, flat rock that served as a sort of cliff on this portion of the land, jutting out of the ground just as there was a mighty dip towards the beaches and actual cliffs. It was not a dangerous spot, but it served as an excellent point for appreciating a view, collecting one's thoughts, or staring blankly in the direction of France.

Generally speaking, of course. He'd never actually tried to determine where France was from this point.

If he had more time, he'd have sat upon the rock and watched the sun dip below the horizon. As it was, he stood there, crossing his arms and trying to force some semblance of relaxation into his frame and mind.

Inhale… Exhale… Inhale… Exhale…

There was nothing of crucial importance that required his activity or direct attention at this very moment. He was in a waiting and watching period, and that would do very well for now. He was only to act as he saw fit, according to the pattern of previous intelligence correspondence, given he did not have a superior pointing him in one direction or the other.

Which meant he could focus his time at the present on his estate lands and farms, which his estate manager would be delighted about. Poor Adams had been acting on his own for far too long and simply keeping Gilles informed on his work and actions. He would love to not be the sole deciding influence for a time.

Gilles could also focus his attention on his daughters, which ought to bring him more joy than he presently felt. He adored his girls to distraction and spent every evening with them before they went to bed, but nothing ever felt like enough. He had to be their father as well as their mother, and he was wholly unequipped to fill the gap left by Heloise. She was the one to fill the girls' minds with imagination, beauty, and joy. He was the one who checked for monsters beneath their beds and saved them from the insects that had found their way into the nursery.

He'd also been the one to lead the family walks along the shore and exploring the coves, but that was something they had not resumed as yet. He could have done. Probably should have done. But exploring the coast by their home and lands seemed a poor prospect without Heloise. And he did not want the girls to feel the loss of their mother more than they already did.

Marie-Claire still asked if Maman could tell her a story from heaven, for pity's sake.

Madeline knew better, even only being one year older, and asked nothing of Maman.

Both of them were starting to ask less and less of Papa, and that broke his heart.

A new governess. How would she handle the life they led here? These sheltered girls whose father forgot a new governess was needed. Who had not yet had a steady feminine influence in the absence of their mother apart from the sweet yet temperamental housekeeper and attentive upstairs maids. Who mingled English and French in their language in a way that not even the natives of Guernsey could understand.

Zut. He was giving the poor governess a mess, indeed. There wasn't anything for it at this point, but he felt it was worth admitting. Perhaps Gilles ought to consider meeting with her in the early days of her time here to explain the situation clearly—apart from his operative work—and apologize for the lapses she would undoubtedly see.

Or should he be the distant, superior, aloof master of the house and let her think whatever she would of him? He had been playing so many roles in the last eighteen months and barely managing any of them.

There weren't that many servants or staff at Coutanche House; would it really matter who he was to the governess?

He felt his shoulders sag more and more with every breath, partially in defeat over his situation, but also, he could admit, with a touch of the relaxation he craved.

This was not worth a cascade of frantic thoughts. It was barely worth cohesive ones.

With a final exchanging of air—a deep inhale and slow exhale—Gilles turned back for the house and bobbed his head in a series of nods, his fingers once again curling and uncurling at his sides. He did not need to worry so much about what he said to the new governess or if he made any apologies. There was no making up for what had led them to this point, but he could do his best starting forward. Which was what the governess would be doing as well, so they were all in the same situation.

Theoretically, at any rate.

Gilles glanced up at the windows on this face of the house and slowed a step. Up in the top right corner, the curtains were open, and a woman stood in the window, looking out towards the sea. The light of the evening was still fairly bright, so he could make out her features and the like without any trouble.

She was not a beauty. Not in the classic sense, at any rate. Her figure was healthy enough, and she seemed to be of a good height. She had a pleasant face, even if it was plain, and the soft smile on her fairly average lips provoked a smile of his own for some reason. He couldn't say with any certainty what color her eyes were, but her hair seemed to be a very dark blonde or a very light brown, and possessed a natural wave to it, if the half-down portion of it was any indication.

She was older than he had expected, but he immediately liked that. The previous governess—the one who had apparently run off with a Guernsey lad—had been young and pretty, so her elopement should not have been much of a surprise. This woman he was seeing was older and undoubtedly filled with more sense, if not wisdom. And she likely was better educated as well. More than that, he had the sense that she would be more maternal towards his girls.

That was what he wished for most of all.

Not a replacement mother for them, but someone who could help with the void Heloise had left that he simply could not manage. A strong, but soft, feminine influence in their lives.

Without meeting her, without hearing her voice, without even knowing her name, he knew this woman would be able to do that.

And with that knowledge, she immediately had all of his confidence, whoever she was.

There was that smile, too. What was she seeing that made her smile so? What was she thinking that allowed such a smile? It was no grin of delight, no polite smile for company, no smirk of cynicism or annoyance. This was a private smile, unobserved but for him, and as gentle as a breeze. Some private joy or contentment brought on such a smile, and she had it there in his house on her first day. On the isolated island of Guernsey.

Of course, she had yet to meet him or his daughters, but he did not anticipate changing her expression much by adding the three of them to the equation.

He was fascinated by this woman, and there was little point in denying it. He'd never spent much time with the previous governesses, but he might just have to make an effort with this one. If for no other reason than to satiate his curiosity and answer the questions he did not yet have words for.

Her eyes suddenly shifted from the distant sea to the ground, and then, as though drawn by force, to Gilles.

Instinct would normally have had him look away at once, but in this case, he held steady. Stared back at her without altering his expression a jot. Let her read what she would out of whatever his face was doing, whatever his posture might tell her, however he might look in this state. She would not know he was the master of this house and should have no discomfort in seeing him. He had no discomfort in seeing her, even knowing who she was.

To his surprise, she did not look away either. He could not even note if her eyes had widened, or her cheeks colored in any particular way. She surveyed him with an equally persistent gaze, everything about her calm and unmoved.

Unflappable.

He liked that.

Yet there was no sense in continuing to stare when they did not know each other, but soon would. Why set up a situation where the governess might be uncomfortable later?

So Gilles simply nodded and continued to walk, forcing himself not to look up at the window again. And he entered the house by a different entrance so it would not be immediately obvious where he was heading. That could either help or hinder the governess, depending on where her mind took her after their silent interaction, but surely she would get a better night of sleep if she did not know that the master of the house had been staring at her without shame.

If she could even tell he was the master.

He glanced down at himself and sighed. He'd gone out in his shirtsleeves, *sans* cravat, and with his weskit entirely unbuttoned. Running a hand over his hair, he could tell it was in complete disarray, which would make him look even more wild than his clothing would allude to. He gave off the impression of being a wastrel to those unfamiliar with the sight of him, and that was certainly not how he wished to be portrayed.

Perhaps, if he made a considerable effort, he could look so altered by the morning that she would not know that the man from the window was the same as the master of the house.

It was worth trying for, at any rate.

He'd never given any governess a second thought, but this one… this one, he already had.

Chapter Three

Coutanche House was one of the loveliest houses Abby had ever set foot in, let alone stayed in. And she had certainly never resided in one so elegant and spacious. She was a Charteris—which counted for a great deal in certain circles—but she was not directly related to those of the vaulted status often so envied. Her family had been rather average in station for several generations, and she had always been grateful to be unremarkable in that regard.

Since becoming an operative and a teacher at Miss Masters's, which had once been a grand estate house itself, she had stayed in a great many places for this mission or that assignment. But none of those places had suited her tastes quite like Coutanche.

The front facade was touched by ivy and wisteria in moderation, giving the silvery grey stone beneath the air of a steppingstone in a pond. The windows glistened brilliantly in any light shone upon them, and the expanse of the building was not enough to be particularly intimidating in grandeur. Simple adornments by way of colonnades, pillars, balconies, and dormers, and less than a dozen windows on three faces of the main house. There was a long extension from the west facade towards the older portion of the house, which, as she understood things, had been made over into more of the servants' quarters, leaving the newer wing to the family.

It presented a degree of privacy that Abby had never seen before, and she'd not even been in residence for a whole day.

Being the governess, Abby had not been certain if she would be in a servants' room or a family room. She had been delighted to find that her room was directly adjacent to the nursery itself, with an adjoining door for convenience. Despite arriving prior to supper, she had not met any member of the family yet. She'd wandered the house before bed last night without encountering a single soul, and it had held a sense of calm as well as one of foreboding.

Mrs. Corbin had been warm and friendly, just as Abby had anticipated from their exchanges in letter, but she was also more of the no-nonsense sort than she had anticipated. Not overbearing, per se, but strict and brisk in her orders. She had insisted that Abby sit for a cup of tea with such force that it had become a matter of obedience to do so. They had talked in jovial tones and Mrs. Corbin had fretted over Abby's fatigue, and particularly over what the trip must have done for her weak leg. Then she had sent her to bed with a brusqueness that would brook absolutely no argument and demanded a hot bath to soothe her frame before she slept.

It was a terrifying combination to have in a woman of authority in a house. There was nothing to do but as she ordered and think back with as much fondness as fear because her intentions were clearly good, and yet…

Well, suffice it to say that Abby would need to tread carefully if she was going to be disrupting this family's life. Mrs. Corbin would probably be her biggest threat if she did. This was *her* family, and no one was going to upset them.

Would Milliner allow Abby to be relocated under a false identity after this assignment to be protected from this terse housekeeper and her unwavering loyalty?

Abby shook her head quickly as she paced slowly in the drawing room where she would soon meet Mr. Bichard and his daughters. She'd had breakfast, and despite having no plans to teach today, was hoping the girls would like to take a picnic with her on the terrace or the grounds. She hadn't explored them yet, but perhaps there was a good place for a picnic that they knew of. She wanted to get a sense of these girls and guide her lessons accordingly. With five years of teaching at Miss Masters's, some of those terms being spent specifically at the Rothchild Academy with the sponsorship students from low classes, she had seen every sort of student imaginable.

Madeline and Marie-Claire were younger than her usual students, of course, but that would only make the teaching experience more fun, in Abby's mind. Meeting Mr. Bichard and asking a few specific questions would determine how structured her teaching needed to be and in what directions he'd prefer she go, all of which was crucial to her time here. She was an operative, yes, but she was also supposed to be a governess, and she was going to do her best by those girls as part of her assignment. They were innocents and should not have anything but her very best, even if she could not stay long.

Hopefully she would not stay long. That would mean her assignment was complete and she had done what she needed to and there was at least some increase in the security of the kingdom against the aims of the Faction.

But that was wishful thinking, and she had never been especially keen on that. She was an optimistic realist, calmly accepting what came and making the best of it.

As she would do here.

She heard the unmistakable sound of young voices from beyond the room and stopped her pacing, turning towards the door in anticipation. She flicked at her skirts, surprised at the sudden burst of nerves.

Children, she reminded herself. These were only children.

But there would be their father.

What would he be like?

The door opened, and two little girls entered, almost perfect images of each other, though one was taller than the other. Both had beautiful golden curls, complexions like china dolls, and wore pinafores of white and blue. The only notable physical difference, size aside, was the color of their eyes. The taller one had dark eyes and the smaller one bright blue, but both pairs of eyes were wide and staring at her.

They were utterly beautiful girls, and Abby could not resist smiling at them to put them at ease, if nothing else. *"Bonjour, mes chéries. Comment vas-tu ce matin?"*

The girls looked at each other, then up at the figure behind them.

Abby had momentarily forgotten that anyone else would be joining them, and followed their gazes quickly, her cheeks flaming with embarrassment.

A jolt of recognition flashed through her body with such a

startling speed and intensity that she could not find a single word at first.

It was the man who had looked at her through the window last evening. The handsome, disheveled man with a piercing gaze and a burdened bearing, whose expression had been incredibly difficult to discern.

He was their father?

His gaze was on her, just as piercing as the night before, and in this light, she could tell that his eyes were a rather muted blue. He was more kempt this morning, but still not perfectly clean-shaven. She did not mind that, not that it was any of her business what he did or did not do about his facial hair or whiskers.

But it was worth noting, for informative purposes, that stubble suited him.

Rather well.

"They do speak English," he said in softly accented English himself, his voice low and almost rumbling. "But French, too. And what the locals say is Guernésiais."

Abby curtseyed quickly, dropping her eyes to the edge of the rug as she did so. "Mr. Bichard, forgive me. I should have introduced myself before speaking to the girls."

"Why?" he asked, his head tilting with the question. "Your attention will be with them, and you greeted them first. I see no fault in this."

"Perhaps," Abby allowed, "but they will not be curious about my surname."

Mr. Bichard made a soft tsking sound. "True. What is it?"

"Chorley, sir. My name is Abigail Chorley." She smiled belatedly and met his eyes again. "I hope you do not mind, sir, but my hope is that the girls will call me Mademoiselle Abby. Or Miss Abby, if you prefer the English. I can teach them in either language. Or both. Whatever you like."

Mr. Bichard looked a little impressed, though it was difficult to tell if it was playacting or genuine. "Indeed? Whatever I like? Well, I am not the student, so I do not suppose what I like is the particular point, is it?" He looked down at his daughters, smiling in a way that crinkled his eyes. "What say you, *ma filles? Anglais ou français?* Or both?"

"Both!" the older one cried with a laugh, the younger one nodding with a slight smile.

He looked back to Abby, gesturing to them. "There you have it. *Les étudiants* have spoken, and so it shall be."

"Very good, then." She clasped her hands and looked at the girls warmly. "My name is Mademoiselle Abby. Will you tell me who you are?"

The older one curtseyed quickly, her dark eyes as bright as her smile. "Madeline, mademoiselle."

The younger one stared at Abby without moving, her expression as indiscernible as her father's had been the night before.

Madeline nudged her with an elbow, and she bobbed a very quick, unsteady, childish sort of curtsey. "Marie-Claire," she recited in a beautiful French accent.

"Papa and I call her Mariette," Madeline informed Abby, as though it would be helpful.

Marie-Claire was already inching towards her father, her fingers gripping at the leg of his trousers.

Abby smiled at her. "Would you like me to call you Mariette as well? Or should that name be just for Papa and your sister?"

"Papa," Marie-Claire whispered as she started to hide her face against him.

"Very well, then. It will be their name for you alone, hmm?" Abby nodded in encouragement, unsure if the girl would even see it.

But Marie-Claire nodded into her father's leg, so that would be good enough for now.

Abby looked at Mr. Bichard quickly. "May I sit, sir?" She gestured to a chair close to Madeline.

He seemed surprised by the question. "Of course."

"Madeline," Abby began as she sat, leaning towards the smiling girl, "do you enjoy having lessons?"

"Sometimes," came her honest reply, her nose wrinkling up. "They can be *ennuyeux*, but learning is *très divertissant* when I like it."

Abby chuckled at the response. "Many things are entertaining when we like them, but we must endure the other times to learn all we must. What is your favorite thing to learn about?"

"Reading," Madeline immediately told her. "I am getting better, am I not, Papa?"

"Oui, ma chérie," Mr. Bichard answered with a warm smile. His eyes crinkled again with the action, and Abby found herself wondering if every smile he bore did the same thing. He ruffled Marie-Claire's curls gently, looking down at her with a fond, patient expression. *"Vas-tu parler, ma petite?"*

Marie-Claire shook her head, but rested her cheek against his leg, her eyes on Abby now.

It was a little progress, which was enough.

Smiling in as a warm a manner as possible, Abby tilted her head at Marie-Claire. "I was hoping we could take a picnic today. I don't know anything about your house or the grounds. Is there a good place to have a picnic?"

Marie-Claire's brow creased very slightly for a moment, and then she nodded firmly.

"Really?" Abby looked playfully delighted. "Where?"

"By the pond," she told her simply.

Abby nodded at the suggestion. "Excellent. If your father agrees, then we'll take a luncheon picnic there."

"I think it sounds *très bien*," Mr. Bichard praised, still absently brushing at Marie-Claire's curls. "Should I come as well?"

"Can you?" Madeline cried with great enthusiasm. "You don't have work to do?"

Mr. Bichard smiled at his oldest, but Abby caught the flash of a different emotion crossing his face just before the smile settled. "Nothing that cannot wait, *ma petite*. And I cannot remember the last time we had a picnic, can you?"

Both girls shook their heads almost somberly, but the smiles they wore were brighter than the sun at noonday.

There was so much love and affection between the three of them. Anyone with eyes would be able to see it, and Abby was delighted by the notion. There was nothing to indicate the girls had any fear of their father or had any significant distance from him, and the very fact that they wanted him to come on the picnic with them was lovely.

But she also had not missed Madeline's question about her

father's work, and she wondered how often her father had used work as an excuse to not do something. Even if it was a legitimate excuse, she knew all too well how easily it could be said and employed. And when there was no other parent to cover the lapses in time and attention, it must seem as though he always had to work and never play. His wish could be to spend all of his time with the girls, but responsibilities did not vanish based on one's wishes or tastes.

Even if those responsibilities involved an evil group of terrorists attempting to overthrow the English and French governments.

The irritation Abby felt at the prospect of this man's true nature and cause burst like a fire in her chest, intense and hot. But with practiced effort, she doused those flames with the icy water of calm determination to see the assignment through. To deliver justice. To use him for the larger purpose of ending the entire Faction.

Which meant pretending he was nothing more than the father of her students, and she was nothing more than an eager governess.

"Should I ask Mrs. Corbin about the picnic fare?" Abby asked Mr. Bichard, uncertain if her thoughts had caused her to miss another exchange between the father and daughters.

He shook his head slightly. "No, I will. Perhaps the girls might give you a tour of Coutanche in the interim. Through their eyes, it might be more interesting, hmm?" He smiled easily, the creases appearing at the corners of his eyes again.

So it was natural, then.

What a distracting prospect.

"It is interesting already, I can assure you." Abby laughed a little and winked at Madeline. "I've never been to Guernsey before, and this house is so large! I am sure I shall become quite lost." She widened her eyes as though she could not believe she was even here.

Madeline giggled loudly and Marie-Claire cracked a wide smile.

The taste of victory was sweet.

"We'll show you *everything*, Mademoiselle Abby!" Madeline insisted with great fervency. "Mariette will come too, won't you, Mariette?"

Marie-Claire nodded obediently, her smile turning almost impish despite the fact that she still clung to her father's leg.

She was going to require some special attention, that one, if Abby wanted her to open up. But shyness wasn't a problem, only a trait, and one that Abby entirely understood. Once Marie-Claire trusted her enough to be less afraid in her presence, her deeper personality would appear, and perhaps show a little bit of a silly side.

If Madeline was as full of life and energy as she appeared, and she and Marie-Claire were indeed close, she suspected they had a great deal of fun and silliness together.

"Lessons?" Marie-Claire asked quietly.

Abby did her best not to beam at the child, not wanting to embarrass her. "Not today, Marie-Claire. I thought you might want to get to know me a little better before I start any lessons. Is that all right?"

Marie-Claire popped a finger in the corner of her mouth, making her look even younger. She smiled widely, her eyes crinkling just like her father's. She nodded without looking away from Abby or ducking into her father's leg.

This little one was the most adorable creature Abby had ever seen, and she was already wanting to sweep her up and playfully cuddle her like an infant just to hear her giggle.

That was possibly more dangerous than her father's smile, but in a very different way.

"How soon is luncheon, Mademoiselle Abby?" Madeline asked her, almost dancing where she stood.

Abby looked at Mr. Bichard with questioning eyes and a slight smile, not entirely sure when any meals took place for the family.

"Not for a little while, Madeline," Mr. Bichard answered with a laugh. "But you could start a tour for your new governess, if you like. By the time you are done, it may be time for our picnic."

Madeline seized Abby's hand and started tugging her away, grabbing her sister's hand as they reached her.

Abby slowed her step, looking at Mr. Bichard earnestly. "I do have some questions about your wishes for the girls' education, sir. When would be an appropriate time to discuss them?"

Mr. Bichard shrugged easily, the motion reminding her of the version of him she had seen the night before, casual and relaxed in his shirtsleeves. "Why not at the picnic? It does not need to be formal. If you cannot tell, mademoiselle, we are not quite the formal family here." He smiled for her now, a touch of pride mingling with the honest delight in it.

And the crinkling eyes seemed to be smiling all on their own.

She had to smile in return; there was no other course.

"I am beginning to sense that, sir," she told him through that helpless smile as the girls pulled at her.

"Mademoiselle Abby, are you hurt? You are walking strangely," Madeline broke in with some concern, but mostly curiosity.

"Madeline," her father scolded at once, though gently, "*tu ne dois pas dire ça.* Apologize, please."

Abby shook her head, letting herself be pulled now. "No, no, it is quite all right. She asked a sincere question based on her observations, and I am not offended." She cleared her throat and smiled at Madeline. "You are very astute, *ma chèrie.* That means you notice things and have a quick mind. On our picnic, I will tell you a very exciting story about my leg and how I came to walk as I do. For now, I will say that I am not hurting at the moment, but I was hurt a long time ago, and now this is simply the way I walk."

Madeline made an O shape with her mouth and nodded quickly. "We have a boy in the stables who walks strangely, but one of his legs is longer than the other. And he runs ever so fast, Mademoiselle. I am still faster, but Papa says I may grow out of that. I do not think I shall."

She continued to rattle on as she tugged Abby completely from the room, making Abby smile with her incessant chatter and details.

Marie-Claire released her sister's hand and came to Abby, taking her free hand without a word, content to silently walk beside her.

Whether that was due to learning about Abby's leg or out of habit when an adult was near was not clear, but she did not mind either way. It was the sweetest gesture, and she decided not to make any sign that something significant had taken place.

But oh, what a beautiful first impression this had been!

Chapter Four

Gilles could not recollect the last time he had spent time out in the grounds on a picnic. He was certain that he and Heloise had done so, and probably even with the girls, but not a single memory of such a thing was coming to mind.

What a tragedy that was.

The girls were delighted to be eating luncheon out in the grounds, a blanket strewn out on the green near the pond for all of them to sit upon. Madeline had chattered animatedly the entire time she had been eating, somehow managing to keep appropriate table manners for her age all the while. Marie-Claire had apparently decided that she was fond of Miss Chorley during the tour of the house, as she sat close enough to her to bump against her leg, side, or arm with every reach for food. If Miss Chorley minded this proximity, she gave no hint of it.

He'd never seen anyone win over his daughters so quickly in his entire life, and they were very amiable girls.

But what astonished him the most was that Miss Chorley seemed to be doing so without exerting an exceptional effort. It was the most natural he had ever seen any governess behave with his daughters, and the most at ease. And the girls were responding with delight and playfulness.

All this within a few hours of meeting her? The future could be promising indeed, if this was the beginning.

"Papa, can we go pick some flowers?" Madeline asked brightly, her golden curls seeming to glow in the streaming sunshine.

Gilles smiled at her and patted her knee. "Of course, *ma fée*. But stay out of the gardens and do not go near the water, *oui?*"

"*Oui,*" she replied primly. She pushed to her feet and brushed at her pinafore. "Mademoiselle Abby, what is your favorite flower?"

Miss Chorley made an obvious effort at thinking. "Wildflowers, probably. And I love all colors."

Madeline put her hands on her hips, huffing slightly. "That is not helpful. All we pick are wildflowers."

Gilles snorted softly, hiding his laugh behind a hand as he stretched his legs out to lounge on the blanket.

Miss Chorley smiled and looked towards the nearby grove of trees carefully. "Why not try to find something… blue? And white. Match your dresses and let us see what you come up with!"

"Yes, Mademoiselle Abby! Come on, Mariette!" Madeline waved her sister along as she started to run, and Marie-Claire was instantly up and trotting along behind her.

Gilles watched them go with fondness, grateful for the fair day that allowed them to be so uninhibited out in their own grounds. It was always good for them to be out of doors, and he was not doing enough to see that they were.

Once they settled into a schedule and routine of sorts with Miss Chorley, Gilles would feel less guilt about spending so much time with his work, but it was not as though he could foist parenting off onto the governess. Nor did he wish to, of course.

He was simply being pulled in so many directions, and without the ballast of his wife, there was nothing to steady him among such tension.

"They are marvelous girls, Mr. Bichard."

Gilles felt his smile spread entirely of its own accord. "*Merci,* Miss Chorley. They are the light of my life."

"I can see that, sir. Am I right in saying that Madeline is six years of age and Marie-Claire is five?"

"Nearly." Gilles glanced over at her, leaning on his elbow. "Marie-Claire is almost five. In a month, she will be."

Miss Chorley was smiling, her cheeks seeming rosier with the motion of her lips. "That explains it."

Gilles knew his own smile went lopsided in his curiosity. "Explains what?"

"On our tour of the house," she began, reaching for another strawberry from the basket, "the girls had a bit of a tiff. Nothing dramatic, but Madeline said that Marie-Claire was still a baby, and Marie-Claire insisted it was not for much longer."

Rolling his eyes, Gilles shook his head, looking towards the grove of trees again, though the shapes of the girls could not be seen. "They are either the best of friends or the worst of enemies. I have never seen closer siblings, but the way they nettle each other at times is truly devious. They know exactly the right places to aim, and yet, in spite of the wounds, they are friends again within moments." He sighed heavily, making a face. "I am sorry they did not behave for you."

"Oh, but they did!" Miss Chorley insisted, shifting her position and drawing his attention back to her. "That little tiff was nothing, truly. Siblings never get along perfectly, especially as children, and to be frank, theirs was the most polite form of familial argument I have ever seen."

"Is that intended to be a compliment?" Gilles asked with a laugh. "They fight nicely?"

Miss Chorley grinned before taking another bite of her strawberry. "Well, they do, sir. And it was all very quick, as you said. Friends once more within minutes. My sisters would have held a grudge for much, much longer, and likely pinched my arm as well. And as for my brothers, well…" She shrugged pointedly.

"Trouble, were they?" Gilles had a hard time imagining that, seeing how calm and contemplative Miss Chorley was. But she had such a way with children, and such an understanding of them, that something in her past ought to have given her that experience.

"There are six of us, all told," she said after a swallow. "And the brothers were determined that the sisters join them in every antic, since we outnumbered them. I am the quietest of the family, but even I was persuaded to take part. It was a loud, rambunctious, lovely way to grow up. Not particularly formal, but I enjoyed it." She smiled almost whimsically then, tucking a finger between her bonnet ribbons at her chin and dragging it along a little.

Gilles watched the motion in a bit of fascination. "Does it chafe? Your ribbons there?"

"Not really, just out of practice with wearing it. I prefer nothing at all on my head if I can help it, but a wide-brimmed hat when I must. I have not fully unpacked everything, so this was all I had to hand." She finished her strawberry and set the end on her plate, chewing quickly, her eyes widening. "But I can assure you, I intend to teach the girls properly. I mean, for them to be proper. Manners and comportment as well as education. My own preferences will not come into it."

"I don't care if they do," Gilles assured her without haste, keeping his tone even. "You seem a very sensible woman as well as accomplished, and you must be qualified enough, or Mrs. Corbin would not have brought you on. I was just thinking myself that I would love for the girls to be out of doors more, as the weather permits. It is a matter of having someone able to escort them to do so, which is difficult with the household staff."

Miss Chorley tsked very softly. "I quite understand. It must be a relief to have me here for that."

Gilles weighed his next words with care, but proceeded anyway. "To be honest, Miss Chorley, I had forgotten that the previous governess had left, and I had no idea it had been three months since she had. I've been very occupied with other things, in spite of all good intentions to the contrary." He trailed off, not seeing the need to confide further in this practical stranger about the deeper feelings of his heart or thoughts in his mind.

He cleared his throat. "So it will be good for us all to have you here and to have the girls in a clear routine. They thrive under such, I believe."

"Decent structure of the day is profitable for most people, adults as well as children. I know it is that way for me." Miss Chorley brushed at her hands and gave him a rather steady look that made her eyes even more startlingly blue than moments before. "Sir, what are your wishes and preferences for the girls' education? What would you like me to focus on? How rigorous would you like the curriculum to be? And how would you like them to spend unoccupied time?"

Gilles blinked in surprise, the questions not necessarily startling, but the idea that he might have considered any such things was. In fact, the notion of contemplating the subject before this moment was positively foreign. Then again, why should it be? Why else had they hired a governess? It hadn't been just due to the loss of Heloise, as their first governess had already been with them at the time, though she'd been more of a nanny than anything else.

And quite frankly, they'd only hired one because Heloise was growing more invested in their work against the Faction and needed some time away from the girls to get more accomplished.

He couldn't exactly tell Miss Chorley that.

But what could he say? As a father, what exactly did he want for his daughters?

He frowned to himself, wishing, not for the first time, that Heloise were here to discuss this with him.

Heloise.

That was it. What sort of woman had Heloise been raised to be? That would be the best of all places to start. He had known her better than anyone in the world and knew what she considered her flaws as well as what she had regretted in her life.

What better guide could he have?

"Everything," Gilles said with a smile, as though he could hear Heloise instructing him. "I want them to learn everything they can. But I want them to be children while they can. They've suffered the loss of their mother, and Mariette may not have much memory of the time before her death, but Madeline does. I do what I can as the only parent, but my wife was the fun and imaginative one. I should like them to have those aspects in their life again."

He glanced up at Miss Chorley and saw her kind, serene expression, and wondered what else lay behind it. "I realize that is not particularly specific as curriculum goes."

Miss Chorley laughed easily, her eyes squeezing shut with the surprise of the moment. "No, sir, it is not. But they are young, as you've said. Perhaps specificity is not required yet."

"Agreed. We have an extensive library, so it would be wise if they were able to read well, and if we can try to instill a love of reading…" He shrugged, sighing. "We cannot dictate tastes, but I would certainly wish for that."

"Oh, I agree, sir," Miss Chorley all but gushed. "Books can open the imagination in countless ways. I should like to encourage imagination and play along with their accomplishment and education, if you'll allow me."

Gilles was nodding before she finished. "Yes, please, Mademoiselle Chorley. I recognize they must eventually learn languages and arithmetic and philosophy, and I don't even know what else. But reading—that is the beginning of everything, is it not?"

"It was for me," Miss Chorley murmured. "I could not draw well, but my governess knew that if she told me I could read when I finished a drawing, I would surely get it done, poor as it might have been."

"Mariette loves to draw, as it happens." He looked towards the grove, smiling almost wistfully at the figures of his daughters on their way back. "As did their mother. She loved…" His heart clenched hard, bringing unbidden tears to his eyes. He lowered his gaze, trying for a swallow to clear his throat, to find the ability to say anything further.

"I am so sorry," came the gentle whisper of Miss Chorley as if by a breeze. "I cannot even imagine the pain."

Gilles shook his head, smiling to himself. "It is more than that. Grief is… complicated, I find. I do miss Heloise very much to this day. But the pain of that is mingled with love, affection, humor, fondness. There is so much pleasure in the memories, even with the longing for her presence and her company. Her laugh…" He began to snicker without warning. "She had the loudest, most unseemly laugh when she was truly amused. Something between chortling and cackling combined with the bellow of a bull. And she snorted."

He heard the choked sound of amusement from beside him and glanced over to see Miss Chorley covering her mouth, her eyes narrowed with restrained mirth. It warmed his aching heart.

"Please, laugh out loud," he told her with a grin. "She certainly did. It echoed in some rooms. We could test the acoustics for concerts by it."

Miss Chorley hunched over, covering her face as giggles escaped her hands.

"I used to save my best stories and jokes for the most inopportune moments," Gilles went on, encouraged by the laughter, "just to get the startled laughter from her."

"That is beastly!" Miss Chorley cried amidst her giggles, dropping her hands. "Oh, she must have been furious!" She immediately sobered, biting her lip. "Sir," she added hastily.

Gilles gave her an almost pitying smile. "Mademoiselle Chorley, please. You do not have to call me 'sir' all the time. I know you are employed here, but it will all be much more comfortable in the house if we are friends. I invite you to speak frankly with me, particularly about the girls. You will see more than I can, and I prefer a direct approach. Don't think of yourself as subservient, I beg of you. We are allies."

Friends? Allies? He wasn't certain what words were tumbling from his mouth or why, but he didn't like the idea of Abigail Chorley being submissive to him. Or to anyone, really. Mrs. Corbin couldn't be helped, as everyone was submissive to her, but as for the rest…

He could use a friend in this house, and Miss Chorley suited him. So far, at least.

A friend among the staff? It was a novel concept for him, but why not? Who was going to complain or care?

She was watching him with those calm, steady eyes, almost a match for the shade of the sky, and there was the slightest curve to her pert lips. "Yes, sir."

Gilles exhaled noisily, shaking his head. "Miss Chorley, really."

"What am I supposed to reply with?" she countered, laughing with the words. "It is only polite, and I can hardly call you by your Christian name, even if we are friends and allies. And it will get very tiresome for both of us for me to say 'Mr. Bichard' every time. I will not say 'sir' as often, but you must permit the occasional usage, or I will sound dreadfully impertinent and defiant."

"I invite you to be impertinent and defiant," Gilles shot back. "I don't believe you could ever be either, in truth, no matter how it feels to you. You have a kinder nature than that."

Miss Chorley's trim brows rose in surprise. "Do I? Already, you think so?"

He nodded once. "I do. Am I wrong?"

Her lips parted to reply, but her attention was pulled in another direction as footsteps sounded in the grass nearby.

"Blue and white, Mademoiselle Abby!" Madeline declared

proudly, holding out the collection of wildflowers for her. Marie-Claire also had a bundle, thrusting it towards her as well.

"Merci, ma chérie." Miss Chorley took the flowers from her and inhaled their scent for a moment. "Shall I turn them into crowns for you?"

"Yes!" Madeline cried, scrambling over Miss Chorley's outstretched legs.

A grimace of pain flashed across the woman's face, combined with an audible hiss and groan. Gilles sat up like a shot. "Madeline! *Sois prudent!*"

"Sorry!" She clapped her hands over her cheeks, looking heartbroken. "I forgot you have a sore leg!"

Marie-Claire stared at Miss Chorley with round eyes, biting down on her lips.

Miss Chorley shook her head, eyes closed, and swallowed. "It's all right, *chérie.* Come here." She opened her arms and her eyes, taking Madeline into her embrace. She waved Marie-Claire over as well, and his youngest also came into her lap, very gingerly.

Gilles relaxed his position only just. "Is it, though?"

She met his eyes and nodded quickly. "Yes, I promise." She ran her hand over Madeline's curls, while Marie-Claire simply snuggled into her. "Shall I tell you how I hurt my leg?"

Madeline sniffled tearfully. "Yes, if it won't hurt your heart, too."

Gilles smiled at his oldest with a surge of tenderness. He watched Miss Chorley raise her eyes heavenward, blinking quickly, her throat bobbing.

"I promise you that it will not hurt my heart. And my leg no longer hurts either. So no more tears, *oui?*"

"Oui," came Madeline's whispered reply.

Her elegant, nimble fingers began to run through Madeline's golden locks in steady motions. "A long time ago, in a quiet corner of England, a young woman was riding a horse to a friend's house. It was very late at night and very dark, and this young woman was riding very recklessly indeed. She hadn't taken the time to ensure everything was fixed properly on the horse, and she was riding astride, which is not at all ladylike."

Gilles listened to her tale intently, reading through the clearly simplified version to try and discern the deeper, perhaps darker, truth. What had Miss Chorley been doing in the middle of the night on a horse that require recklessness? She did not seem the sort to do anything reckless, no matter what time of day it was, but recklessly riding a horse…

That seemed even more far-fetched.

What had driven her to that? Going to a friend's house, she said? In the middle of the night? Was it a lover she had been riding to? There was no other explanation, in his mind, and for whatever reason, he did not care for it.

At all.

"I was riding so fast and so hard," she continued in a strong, yet somehow distant voice, "and it was so dark that I did not see certain hazards in my path. I was so fatigued, you see. I was not very well, and… I fell from my horse, who, you will remember, was going very fast, indeed. I hit the ground so hard that my leg broke in several places."

Madeline whimpered just as Gilles grimaced, the image of Abigail hitting the dark, cold ground with intensity an unwelcome one. And if she had been unwell at the same time…

She pressed a soft kiss to Madeline's hair and tightened her hold on Marie-Claire. Was that to comfort them or herself for the story she was telling?

"It hurt very badly," she murmured, her eyes settling somewhere around the picnic basket, but unfocused. "So badly I fell asleep. And when I next woke, I was far away from where I had fallen. There were no doctors, and so my leg did not heal well. And now it does not work as well as it once did. It tires easily, it is weaker than the other, it does not bend well, it is sensitive when eager girls climb upon it." She tickled Madeline's side as she said this, making her giggle and squeal.

Right when Madeline might have felt another burst of guilt and tears.

Remarkable intuition, and compassion.

Abigail giggled, too, taking a moment to do the same with Marie-Claire. "But I can stand. I can walk. I can ride, if I am careful. I don't run, but that does not trouble me. I can play all sorts of games and dance some of the dances. My leg will pain me afterwards and for the next day or two, but I am always well. Always. Because bodies are strong, and they are made to heal. Did you know that?"

Madeline nodded while Marie-Claire shook her head, making Gilles smile. "Remember, *ma fée,* when you scraped your knee?"

Marie-Claire looked at him, bobbing her head in a nod.

He gestured a semi-shrug. "Your body did that without you saying so. It healed the wound all on its own."

"Oh," she said in her sweet little voice. She looked up at Abigail with a small smile. "Now I know."

Abigail chuckled and tapped Marie-Claire on the nose. "Indeed, *ma chérie.* Now you know!" She smiled at Gilles, which made him smile. Then she cleared her throat and picked up the flowers. "So, with these flowers, we shall make crowns for you girls."

Gilles watched her as she worked, unable to rid himself of the smile. She was a natural with them, and they were already devoted to her. But it was more than that. Abigail was like a breath of fresh country air when one has been choked by city air for too long. She was not quite sunshine, but there was a brightness to her. And the story she had just told… There had to be more to it than that. More misery. More danger. More chance of death.

More darkness.

And she had endured it all and could still be that refreshing air.

It was a marvelous thing, and he wanted to understand it. He wanted to know all of it. He wanted to learn how to capture even a portion of that for himself.

And he wanted, most of all, to understand why she had suddenly become Abigail to him instead of Miss Chorley.

For Abigail she now was, and there was no going back.

Chapter Five

The Bichard girls were up to something, and Abby's curiosity was getting the better of her. They had been quiet, docile, and perfectly obedient in their lessons, and considering how the last two days had gone, that was an aberration.

Not that they were mischief makers. They were angels most of the time. Angels with loud opinions, fervent wishes, and unbridled passions, as well as very active imaginations. All of which Abby loved, but it did make the uninteresting work far more difficult to get through.

Today, the weather was beautiful and fair, which made remaining in the schoolroom less than inviting. It was a common issue with her students in Kent, but they were at least old enough to have developed restraint in word and deed.

Madeline and Marie-Claire, on the other hand…

Abby had caught them looking out the windows repeatedly, but they had said nothing. Not a word about escaping or going for a walk or picking flowers, all of which they had asked for in the days previous when the weather had only been half so lovely. The fact that they were not saying anything at all on the finest day for weeks was more suspicious than anything else.

There was nothing to complain about when it came to the Bichards or living at Coutanche. Truly nothing. The house was quiet constantly, apart from the girls being the children they were, and Mr. Bichard never interfered with lessons, but checked in with his daughters frequently at regularly scheduled intervals. Usually morning before lessons, at family supper, and then at bedtime, but there had been the picnic a few days before, and yesterday he had surprised them all with teatime during a break in lessons. The girls had been delighted by the surprise, and they had asked for stories of his childhood.

According to Mr. Bichard, this was not an unusual request.

He had grown up in Quimper, on the coast of France, ships and beaches and festivals a regular part of his memories and stories. Cousins, too, and mischievous adventures with them seemed to be a recurring theme, which Abby found endearing.

Not that her employer should be in any way endearing, but to know that this bookish, softspoken, attentive father had an active childhood himself was certainly promising for her aims with the girls. To see them continue to flourish in the world of imagination and light. To be free of the shadows that Madeline still bore at night, but Marie-Claire only had rarely. To have the freedom to become whomever they were, however the world would let them—or to challenge those very restrictions.

They were not her daughters, and she did not intend them to be. Every girl Abby taught was a vessel for those same hopes, dreams, wishes. Everything that Abby's life could not be, she poured into them, whether operative or lady. She could not help herself; they deserved anything they wished for themselves, so long as it was good and could not harm anyone.

The girls at the Rothchild Academy could not usually find the light and innocence for true imagination of their age, not with the lives they had lived up to that point and the horrors they had endured. But most were able to rid themselves of the worst of shadows, and that was usually enough.

With the Bichard girls, there were fewer shadows, but the ones they had were deep. However, young as they were, there was a chance of restoring them to true childhood and its wonders yet.

A very soft, very high-pitched clearing of a throat brought Abby round from the windows looking out towards the sea.

Perhaps it was she who had gotten distracted by the beauty of the day rather than her students.

"Apologies, *mes filles,*" she said with a smile, as both girls looked at her with curious, eager eyes. "Have you finished your letters?"

"Yes, Mademoiselle Abby," they recited in sisterly unison with perfection.

Sheer perfection.

Abby narrowed her eyes at them both, trying desperately not to smile. "Let me see them."

Obediently, the girls turned their parchment pages to her, upon which childish versions of letters were laid out in neat rows beside the original letters she had written for them.

Exactly how she wanted.

Her eyes raised to the girls, the urge to smile more compelling than ever. "What exactly are you girls up to? You have some scheme in mind, and somehow it is tied to pristine behavior."

The sisters looked at each other before giggling in the manner she had anticipated dealing with all afternoon.

She folded her arms, letting herself smile now. "What is it?"

"We thought you might let us go outside," Madeline said with a shrug, grinning at her. "To the beach."

"If we were good enough," Marie-Claire added swiftly. "And did our lessons."

Abby looked from one to the other with true amusement. "You decided that I might be more amenable to going out to the beach if you behaved very well?"

Their nods were not quite identical in pattern or form, but the ripple of them was delightful.

"If you did your lessons well and did all that I asked without distraction or complaint?" Abby pressed.

"Yes, Mademoiselle Abby." Their voices were once again in perfect unison, in note, tone, and cadence. A particular, sisterly unison that no other creatures on Earth could replicate.

And it was too much. It was adorable and conniving and brilliant and, above all else, utterly irresistible.

Sighing as though relieving herself of a great weight, Abby folded her arms. "Oh, why not?"

The girls cheered, loudly and exuberantly, throwing their hands up into the air in victory.

Abby picked up their pages and tucked them into a book that she then set aside. "Come on, we need to make sure we have the proper footwear and hats. No one wants a pink nose and cheeks before bed, do they?"

They bolted from their seats and darted for the nursery on pattering feet, their giggles unfettered in their entirety. Abby went to her room, changed from slippers to boots, and brought out her wide-brimmed hat. She hadn't been down to the beaches yet, but the girls were eager and excited, and Abby suspected outings there were part of their favorite activities, so they would know the way.

She had not played at a beach for many years. Even then, it was perhaps only twice. She had never taken the time to simply enjoy the coast in Kent near the school. With her leg, what would be the point of it? Strolling along the water's edge might have been a romantic idea, but damp sand would be a troublesome surface for her. Dry sand was just as difficult, but with the children, it could be all right. Stony ground was tricky as well, whether it was dry or wet.

There was really not a good version of walking along a beach with an injury such as hers, but the girls would have a pace she could cope with, and if she truly minded her steps, she would not even feel a twinge of discomfort.

And these were her most stable, protective boots, so it was her best option to safeguard herself.

The girls had their own tiny boots in hand as she moved into the nursery, so she quickly helped put them on and tie the laces. When they had found their hats, the three of them made their way down the stairs and into the entrance hall.

"Now, girls," Abby said as she turned to face them, sweeping her eyes from one to the other quickly. "Do we have everything needed for a trip to the beach? Be truthful, please."

They looked at each other, at their boots, their hats. Then they looked at Abby and nodded with a somberness that did not suit the nature she had come to expect from them in recent days.

It was clear that there were particular rules for such outings, and the girls knew them.

"All right, then," Abby said slowly. "Do we need to tell Mrs. Corbin that we're going, perhaps?"

Madeline scowled, but Marie-Claire nodded very fervently, her wide blue eyes showing all of her young innocence in her response.

Not a hint of the previous scheming in it, despite what her older sister might have wished for. No duplicity or deceit.

At what age did that all change?

"Then let's make it quick, hmm?" Abby grinned and winked at them, which seemed to settle Madeline's discontent rather efficiently.

It was a quick walk down the two corridors to Mrs. Corbin's sitting room, and the housekeeper insisted they take along a basket just in case they got hungry by the seaside.

With the added weight and slight complication of something on her arm, Abby's gait was even more altered and taxing than usual. That would make matters more difficult when they got to the coast, but she should be able to manage.

They had exited the house from the kitchen side of things, though the girls walked towards the front of the house anyway, so that must be where their known path lay. In an ideal world, Abby would have walked beside them, if not ahead of them, but she no longer lived in an ideal world. She lived in a crippled one, and while that was fine for being a teacher in a finishing school, where the floors were even and stable, it was proving more trying here.

Her leg was not supposed to be an impediment on this assignment. She would need to push herself hard to make sure that it wasn't.

"And where are you three going?" asked a low, softly accented voice that seemed to carry a smile in its tone.

Abby smiled herself at its sound and looked around, unsure where it was coming from.

"Papa!" the girls cried as they saw Mr. Bichard step into view from the front facade of the house, dressed in the perfect attire of a country gentleman, even if his cravat was a trifle loose and he wore no hat. His daughters ran to him and hugged him hard, though they had just seen him that morning.

He hugged them a moment and offered a smile and nod to Abby in greeting. "Mademoiselle Chorley."

"Mr. Bichard," she replied with a quick bob and a smile in return.

He looked down at his daughters with questioning eyes. "Who is going to answer my question?"

Marie-Claire, bless her, raised her hand as though they were in lessons.

Mr. Bichard fought a smile, his eyes dancing as he looked down at his youngest, and Abby was hard pressed to keep her smile contained as it was. "Yes, Mariette?"

"We were going down to our beach," she recited perfectly. "We have hats and boots and a basket."

Madeline audibly grumbled as she glared at her younger sister, which startled Abby. What would be so wrong with Marie-Claire telling their father the plan?

"I see," Mr. Bichard said solemnly. "And what is the rule for going down to the beach? Madeline, I believe it is your turn to answer a question."

Sensing she had been played for a bit of a fool, Abby tuned in to the conversation with more interest, forcing her expression to remain free of emotion.

Madeline swept one foot along the ground, keeping her head down. "We have to tell you that we wish to and go with an adult."

"And why is that?"

"So we are safe," she said on a longsuffering sigh. "But we are going with Mademoiselle Abby, Papa!"

Mr. Bichard nodded in agreement, the corners of his mouth twitching. "Indeed, and that would be well, except I suspect Mademoiselle Chorley has not been down to the beach yet and therefore does not know the way there nor back home. If there had been danger, she would not know where to go for help."

Abby closed her eyes in mortification, seeing the issues at hand laid out before her like the blatant display of an unaccomplished musician within the first notes of a song.

What had she been thinking? Of course their father should have been informed! Of course she ought to have ensured she knew the way to the beach and back before agreeing to this! Of course she should not have been persuaded into an activity by children when she was still a stranger!

Idiot. She would be fortunate to not lose her position. Then what would they do about the mission?

"So what do you have to say for yourselves?" Mr. Bichard asked, setting his hands at his hips.

Abby shook her head slowly. "Sir, I can only ap—"

He met her eyes at once and cut her off with a quick flick of his fingers. "Not you, Mademoiselle Chorley. Them." He looked down at the girls. "Hmm?"

"Je suis vraiment désolé, Papa," both of them murmured obediently, their faces perfectly glum with the apology.

Impossibly, Mr. Bichard was now smiling in truth, his eyes crinkling. *"Tout va bien.* Shall we go down to the beach together now?"

His daughters gasped in utter delight and hugged him tightly, squealing as they did so. *"Merci, Papa!"*

"Go on, find the path, but don't go down it," he directed, gesturing towards the direction of the water.

The girls dashed off immediately, leaving Abby alone with her employer.

She swallowed hard. "Sir, I am so sorry, I didn't—"

He sighed heavily and gave her a hard look. "Mademoiselle Chorley, I have already said that I did not need an apology from you, and I do not require one now. I am the one who did not take the time to show you the safest way to the beach, nor explain to you the rules I have for going there. The girls, however, know exactly what is expected of them. Please accept my apology for not giving you all of the requisite information to allow you outings to the beach when you wish it."

"No apology necessary," Abby murmured as she started to follow the girls. "And really, going to the beach at all was their idea. I simply agreed to it."

"And what did they do to earn such an outing?" he asked, falling into step beside her.

Abby laughed very softly. "Behaved? Not that they do not do so normally, but they were quiet, docile, perfectly obedient angels all morning. Which, of course, made me suspicious."

"Indeed, you were right to be so." He chuckled once. "Very suspicious of them. But it cannot be helped when the day is like this. And I have not taken them to the beach in some time."

"They seem to love going there," Abby remarked as the girls waited impatiently for them at the head of the path.

Mr. Bichard nodded as he walked, his eyes also on his girls.

"They do. And we used to come down often with their mother, but it has all been rather sporadic since her passing. And lately, I haven't thought of it much. I've more of a head for business where the sea is concerned than the entertainment of my daughters. Without someone else to take them, they have probably felt trapped in the house."

Abby wrinkled up her nose at the idea. "I don't know about that. There are several other things to do in the house and about the grounds, if one is creative enough."

He made a low sound of amusement beside her. "You presume anyone in my household has a creative mind besides you, mademoiselle. Our staff is not large, and the demands of Coutanche take up most of their time." He laughed again, this time almost heartily. "And what is the point of having a house within walking distance of the beach if one cannot visit often?"

"You may have a point there," she allowed with a small laugh herself. She smiled as the girls jumped up and down in excitement, almost to them now. "They are waiting so well."

"The path is a steep one," Mr. Bichard explained. "They know it must be done under supervision, even if it is stable." He drew up a moment, putting a hand to her arm. "I do apologize, Mademoiselle Chorley. I did not consider… your leg…"

Abby dipped her chin for just a moment. "I ought to be fine, so long as it is not a slippery path. Slow, but fine. Please, do not be concerned. I've learned how to adapt to many things."

He searched her eyes and face for a moment, then nodded, which made her breath come just a touch easier. "Very well. Will you require assistance?"

Smiling, she shook her head. "No, sir. But if you and the girls might wait for me at the bottom?"

"Of course." He took the basket from her arm without a word, nodding once more. "Please, take your time. The path is usually perfectly traversable and without any risk, but the girls would run it and possibly do injury, so it—"

"Sir," Abby overrode with a slight smile as his reassurances became rambling. "I can promise you, I will be fine. Please, go with the girls."

His smile was also slight in return, and he nodded a little before moving to the girls and insisting they go slowly. She watched as he took Marie-Claire's hand and began down the path with all the caution of a concerned parent, and let her smile fade as she moved to the path herself.

Abby was not worried about the venture; she had managed hilly trails of various inclines before. What she truly was uncertain of involved the man who was her employer.

She had yet to determine how to properly investigate anything taking place in his life. He had no discernable pattern to his days or his time, and he had yet to leave the house since her arrival. Short of exploring the house and the grounds late at night, she wasn't certain how anything would get done. And with her being a governess during the day, she was entirely unaware of the post arriving from day to day.

And really, he did not seem the sort of man desperate for a wife, nor to wish to have anything to do with Society. But then, it would not exactly befit a man to admit any such thing to a woman in his employ.

She was going to need some clue as to where to start looking, what to start looking for, and what could possibly convince a man as gentle and kind as Mr. Bichard seemed to be to have a young woman kidnapped for his marriage.

But she had met pleasant people before who were privately the worst sort of villains. It happened all the time, and here would be just another example. Even cruel men were capable of loving their children sometimes.

And what of the late Mrs. Bichard? Everything she had heard from her employer about her could have been a complete fabrication. She would need to verify details with Mrs. Corbin or one of the maids; at least then she might have some inkling about Mr. Bichard's true feelings regarding marriage in general, as well as his first one.

Starting down the path, Abby found the ground relatively even and well-worn, packed enough to keep her from slipping on a loose patch, even if the grade was steeper than she liked. It was awkward going, having to step down with her bad leg first, as it couldn't bend well, and its weakness did not permit a particularly stable base for herself.

None of this was revelatory, of course. She had tested her legs to their limit over the years in her desperation to be of better use to the Convent and to Milliner. It had always led to disappointment, despite any notes of progress.

She wanted to be as she had been, not as she was. There was no victory in progress if she was not restored to her past strength and abilities.

She was walking down an incline to the beach, for pity's sake. She would have sprinted down it once, laughing hysterically at the propulsion added to her speed and lengthening her strides. She'd have tumbled to the ground by the end and thought nothing of it. Might have even done so again for the thrill.

But now…

Abby glanced down the path to gauge the remaining distance and saw, with a jolt, Mr. Bichard waiting for her. Watching her every step. His expression was taut, and his eyes missed nothing. Was he now noticing how significant her impediment could be and debating on sending her off? Was he offended to have hired on such a cripple? Was he even now weighing the trouble of finding a new governess for his daughters?

What would she tell Milliner if that happened?

Chapter Six

It was more difficult than Gilles imagined, watching Abigail struggle down the path. She showed no sign of pain, but the maddening pace of her descent, the way her leg shook when she took another step, the inability to bend that leg enough to let her strong one lead…

He saw her eyes flick to him and noted the creases forming in her brow.

Concern. Why should she be concerned? His eyes darted across her features and noted the faint rise of color in her cheeks.

Ah. Embarrassment, then. Perhaps shame.

That was unnecessary. There was nothing wrong with her in any true sense, and a slow gait was certainly no cause for irritation or impatience when it could not be helped. But he could understand how it might cause her to feel vulnerable, especially when she was being so carefully observed. He did not intend to cause her discomfort by watching; he only wanted to ensure that she was safe.

Once she was by his side, he'd tell her so.

He glanced over his shoulder to check on the girls, both of whom were picking up small pebbles and tossing them back into the water with cheerful cries of something he couldn't make out. Knowing their imaginations, it could be anything.

Gilles returned his attention to Abigail, who had only a few more steps to go. He scanned her face once more for any signs of pain, but there were none. It was a strange relief to know that not every step was agony for her, but it did nothing to keep him from wanting to reach out and help her manage every single one she took.

Not that she needed his help. She managed perfectly well, all things considered.

But he wanted to help.

Badly.

He caught her short exhale as she took the final step down and smiled for her.

She did not smile back. "Sir," she began in a low, rushed tone, "I hope you don't think—"

"I don't know what you are going to say, Mademoiselle Chorley," Gilles overrode in a louder voice, keeping his smile in place, "but it had better not be an apology or some belief that what I have just witnessed has tarnished the opinion of you that I might have had this morning."

Abigail's mouth fell open, then she closed it, swallowing.

"If my close observation of you made you in any way uncomfortable," he went on, lowering his voice and stepping closer, "then I am sorry. I simply wanted to ensure you made your way down safely. That was my concern. Nothing more, nothing less. And now that you are down with us, I think, perhaps, we should walk, don't you agree?"

She was silent one moment more, then nodded. "Yes, sir."

Such a simple, almost clipped reply, and her color was still high. Was she angry with him now? Abigail did not seem to be the sort to anger easily, and yet…

"Mes filles!" Gilles called to the girls. "Come, this way."

Madeline and Marie-Claire darted over to them, each taking one of Abby's hands as the four of them walked together.

"Now what were you two doing over there?" Abigail asked them with pointed curiosity, her voice far brighter and more playful with them than it had been with him.

"Freeing the snails!" Madeline cried with pure glee.

"Snails?" Abigail repeated. "You were throwing snails into the ocean?"

"They were pebbles," Marie-Claire told her somberly. "We pretended they were snails."

Abigail made a dramatic sound of relief. "That is very good to know. I don't believe real snails enjoy being thrown anywhere."

The girls giggled in near-perfect unison, making Gilles smile further. There was nothing quite like hearing laughter from his daughters, and Abigail had a knack for bringing it out of them.

Their cheerful conversation continued as they walked to the cove and caves almost directly in line with Coutanche House, their usual spot for any beach outings. Gilles set down the basket and shucked off his coat, waving the girls over to him.

"Remember the rules?" he asked them as he untied their boots and helped remove their stockings.

Both nodded without a word.

"Tell me," he pressed, setting the items aside.

"Only walking," Marie-Claire began, her brow puckering. "No water above the knees."

"Stay together," Madeline went on, "and don't go into the caves without an adult."

Fighting a grin, Gilles nodded in approval. *"Très bien, les petites.* Go play."

The girls dashed over to the water's edge and started walking into it, squealing as the cold water touched their skin.

Gilles turned and saw Abigail watching them with a smile, making no move to approach the water herself.

She looked at him, and her smile faded just a little.

He would not pretend that was not disappointing.

"Are you not going to venture into the water, Mademoiselle Chorley?" he asked, keeping his tone light and easy.

Abigail shook her head. "No, sir."

"May I ask why?"

Her jaw tightened, and again a blush rose on her cheeks, stretching almost to her small, perfect ears. "I am… uncomfortable removing my shoes. When my feet can be seen by others."

Gilles frowned at her, his mind turning her words over several times. "Because of decency, or…?"

"Scars, sir," she bit out. "My right foot has unsightly scars, just as the entire leg does. Horrible, pinching, restricting, contracting scars as far as the eye can see. Something out of a sensational novel, perhaps, or the depraved imagination of a medical man, but very real upon each layer of my skin. Propriety protects me in most respects, but here…” She trailed off, keeping her eyes on the sea, her throat working. “I will not frighten the children with the sight, and I am reminded enough of the scars in private, so there is no need to reveal them otherwise.”

Taking a moment to consider his words, Gilles wet his lips. “You need not be concerned on our account, Mademoiselle Chorley. If you wish to keep them covered, then, of course, do so. But if you think it might change the way my daughters or I see you, I can assure you it will not.”

“How can it not?” Abigail hissed, her voice choked. Her eyes, the color of the sea itself, began to shimmer with unshed tears. “How can watching my struggle down the path or my scars not change the way I am seen? It has changed everything else in my life. I do not wallow in self-pity, sir, but that does not mean I do not feel mortification and shame about my condition. I see the way others look at me when I walk. When I navigate stairs. When I cannot run or ride or dance. You may tell me as many times as you like that you are only concerned for my safety, but do you know how much I wish no one would look? That no one would watch? That even those with the best of intentions did not see me as a creature requiring concern?”

There was no fair way to answer her series of questions. Of course he did not know. Of course he could not perfectly understand. Of course he could not completely comprehend her experiences since her injury had occurred and rendered her so impaired.

But he did want to ensure her safety. He did look at her with concern. He did want to help her. He could see her difficulties and only wanted to help.

Was that such a great sin against her?

He looked away, focusing on the sea, as she was, wondering what to say and how to say it. He heard her short exhale, followed by a sniffle.

“I apologize, sir. I should not have lashed out. It is not customary for me to be so sensitive on this subject, and I can assure you, it will not happen again.”

Such a formal apology, and so stiffly expressed.

Why shouldn’t she occasionally rage about her plight?

“You told us on our picnic,” Gilles began slowly, “that you were riding to a friend's house late at night rather recklessly. That your saddle was not secure, and the like. Having ridden recklessly at night myself, Mademoiselle Chorley, I understand the setting well. But if you might indulge someone with a bit more idea of the dangers than my daughters, how did your injury prove so very disastrous?"

She said nothing to this, and Gilles glanced at her, wondering if he would see anger or offense in her face.

He saw neither.

Her eyes were lowered in thought, but her brow clear. He saw her throat bob once, caught a slow blink.

"I was fleeing," she finally said very softly. "You must not ask me why. As I told you, I was fatigued and unwell, but fit enough to ride, I thought. The road was heavily wooded and unfamiliar to me. I was riding to a friend's home, but it was not a usual path. It was a cloudy night, so there was no moonlight. It had rained recently, so the terrain was soft and slick. My horse was perfection, sleek and skilled at all manner of riding. But in fleeing as I was, my attention was not where it ought to have been. I attempted a jump over a fallen tree, not seeing the lower hanging branches just above…"

Gilles winced in anticipation and sympathy, knowing what would surely follow.

Abigail cleared her throat. "I was swept off of my horse with tremendous force, and rendered breathless by the impact, but I distinctly remember the thought of trying to protect my head from hitting the ground. I attempted to turn myself as I fell, thinking landing on my side would be better. But the very tree I had tried to jump now lay exactly where I was falling, and it was that tree that caught my fall."

He bit back a groan, the vision of such a collision churning his stomach in an almost sickly manner.

"I've never heard such sounds," she whispered, shaking her head as her eyes raised to the sea. "And from my own body, too. Snapping and cracking… And I did hit my head after all, though my leg took the brunt of the force. Broken branches stabbing into my thigh and foot… Everything goes very hazy in my memory then; the pain was so overwhelming. But I do recall a strange protrusion of white through my lower leg, dripping a horrid sort of sludge."

Gilles stared at her in horror, trying to imagine the scene as she described and finding his mind unwilling to consider it. "How were you recovered?" he asked in a harsh whisper.

She shook herself and swallowed hard. "I have no idea. I awoke in some cottage four days later, having raged in fever and not well enough to lift my head. But thank God I was unconscious, as I understand the resetting of bones to be utter torment. Then the wounds became inflamed, so I was feverish again." She sighed and shrugged her shoulders. "I was there for two weeks before I was well enough to return to my family. The healing was slow and agonizing at times, but heal I did. Walking is a miracle, I am told, but it does not feel miraculous. Keeping my leg was apparently miraculous, but it feels like a drag and chain. Please don't mistake me, I am grateful, but…"

"But in being as able as you are," Gilles murmured, "you are left with the memory of what you once were, and the longing for that overwhelms the gratitude of what you were spared."

Abigail looked at him in surprise, her pale eyes searching his with an almost frantic air. "Yes," she breathed. "How did you know?"

How did he know? He wasn't certain, but he thought of his loss of Heloise, the fever that had carried her away and how it had not touched anyone else in the house. Of the state of France, his beloved homeland, and what it could have been rather than what it was becoming. Of the Faction, even, where there had once been such promise and such glorious ideals, and now only the darkness that almost resembled the Revolution. Of his once close association with his brother, in heart and mind and purpose, and yet now they were practically strangers as Gaston sank further into the dark depths of the Faction and Gilles stayed removed from it.

In so many respects, he mourned for what was lost rather than treasured what remained.

He could not do more than he was with France and the Faction, and he was not certain what could be done in regard to his brother without risking his tenuous connection with England. But he could treasure his girls and the fact that there had been no sickness or death there. He could love them and raise them as Heloise had wanted and how they had planned.

And he could ensure that he had the most capable, impressive, worthy woman as their greatest feminine influence.

He was quite certain he was standing beside that very creature now. There was no one like her in his acquaintance, and he could almost feel Heloise prodding him with her elbow in his side. She'd have adored Abigail and done everything in her power to keep her there with them on Guernsey. In their household. In their lives. She'd have adopted her, if possible, and seen to her every comfort and need.

He could see that perfectly laid out before him as though it had been one of their lengthy discussions, but without Heloise here, with having her gone so long, there was something else as well. Something that flickered warmth within him.

Something…

"Sir?"

An idea struck Gilles then, and he smiled softly as it unfurled in his mind like an ancient scroll. He turned to Abigail and gently took her upper arm. "Come with me."

Her brow creased, darkening her eyes to a peculiar shade of grey. "But the children…"

He nodded at her concern. "We aren't going far, and we will still be able to see them. Trust me."

The storms in her eyes cleared, her skin smoothing, and the smallest of smiles quirked at the corners of her mouth. "All right."

Gilles had not anticipated the burst of pleasure he felt at her acquiescence, but did his best to tamp down any sort of reaction. He started leading her over to the caves nearby, eyeing the ground beneath their feet. At this time of day, the water was not reaching the caves, but it certainly did so whenever the tide came in. A few of them flooded entirely during storms, but there had not been any of late. The spring tides were in, so water was higher than at other times of the year, but there were several hours yet before the caves would be any sort of danger.

"Here," he murmured softly, gesturing to the first cave and leading her into it. This one was large and wide at its entrance, narrowing quite markedly after the first rise of ground, but they would not be going far.

He stopped them both at the rise and gestured to a pool of water just in front of them.

"This," Gilles told her, his voice echoing in the enclosed space, "is a warm spring. It overflows and cools with a high tide, but never drains entirely. The water flows from cracks in the earth and underground rivers. Not quite as impressive or sought after as the ones the Romans capitalized on in Bath, but perhaps just as useful."

"Useful?" Abigail repeated, tilting her head at him. "How so?"

Gilles looked at her fully, smiling wide. "It is not especially deep, Mademoiselle Chorley. And it could prove very beneficial to you and your leg if you should like to try and improve things. There are no promises, of course, but the nature of water and the warmer temperatures here rather than in the sea might allow you to unlock some of the hindrances your injuries have left you with."

The more he spoke, the wider her eyes became, and by the time he finished, she was staring at the pool with slightly parted lips.

There was no sound now but for the faint echoes of the waves on the shore outside and a dripping from deeper within the cave.

Abigail swallowed, licked her lips, then said in a shaking voice, "I hadn't thought… I had not considered…"

"That there could ever be an improvement?" Gilles offered gently, taking her arm once more. "I have no doubt that everything was done for you, but I am from a coastal town in France, Mademoiselle Chorley. There is very little that has not been attempted with the waters there, and many, many myths that have their roots in truth. Even if you do not find lasting increases to your motion, you can at least be assured that it will help your pains and allow you better movement while you are in it."

Her breath seemed to pant from her lips then, and he turned her to face him, afraid he had gone too far, said too much, assumed incorrectly… That he'd somehow hurt her in this.

But she was smiling at him, her eyes bright even in the lowered light of the cave. "Thank you, Mr. Bichard. This could be… wonderful." She swiped at a pair of tears escaping her eyes and laughed. "Is it safe to come down here alone?"

Gilles grinned at her and turned to face the spring again. "Yes, so long as the tides are low. The ground, as you see, is quite secure, and the water should not rise above your arms in any portion of the spring. So long as you have the strength to climb out, you will be perfectly safe. And just there by that outcropping? There is a slant to the ground, so it may well be your easiest point of entry and exit."

Abigail shook her head as she looked where he pointed. "However did you find this place, sir?"

"Oh, Heloise and I explored every inch of the grounds when we made our purchase of this place," he said on a sigh, thinking back to the delightful memories of exploring the cove and caves with his wife. "She rather enjoyed coming to the spring when she was with child and growing uncomfortable with it…" He felt heat rush into his cheeks as he trailed off. "Forgive me, I ought not speak of such things."

"I have sisters, sir," Abigail quipped without shame. "I know all about the discomfort of childbearing, aside from personal experience with it. I can perfectly see how the warm spring would benefit her in that condition." She hummed softly, the emotion behind it unclear to his ears. "Now I must only ensure I can find my way back here when I come."

"Ah, yes," Gilles said with a grin as he started walking back towards the cave opening with her. "I can help you with that. In fact, I will show you an easier path to get down here, one with less of an incline. It is a bit farther on, but might be worth it for your comfort. Be sure you come in the mornings, of course, as the tide is safest for the caves then. And I hope that you will feel no guilt for taking a morning to come here rather than teach lessons. I insist that, if this interests you, it becomes a priority. The girls will be perfectly well with a morning of play once a week."

"I have just the thing to entertain them on those days," Abigail replied quickly, her voice stronger now and filled with energy and light. "Paper dolls. I brought some with me for them and have yet to show them off. It could be the only time they play with the dolls. That is, when I come down here for swimming and exercise. And it will not take an entire morning, of course. I shall have to begin slowly and gradually, as with any sort of training. Else I may do myself more harm than good, and then where would we be?"

She laughed a merry, throaty sort of laugh that he had yet to hear from her. He'd heard snickers and giggles with one thing or another, but this… This dance of sound was as natural and pure as the crashing of the waves on the shore and the purr of the water as it slunk back out to its mother sea. Her eyes crinkled as she squeezed them shut in her mirth and her lips took on a rosier hue that made them quite captivating.

He'd never paid attention to her mouth before, nor the sound of her voice, but suddenly both were imprinted in his mind as surely as a branding. And the motion of her throat as she laughed…

Gilles focused his attention on the sea ahead of them as they emerged from the cave and forced himself to make some semblance of a chuckling sound so as to avoid the odd detection of his shifting emotions.

"Indeed, Mademoiselle Chorley," he said around his false laughter, his pulse beginning a frantic pounding in his throat. "Where would we be?"

Chapter Seven

Nighttime wanderings at Coutanche House were not for the faint of heart.

Despite the many dangers she had faced as an operative, despite the training she had received, despite her once reckless nature, Abby found herself wincing with every creak of the floorboards beneath her feet. Surely, there had never been a floor more prone to telling tales than this one, and her heavy-laden leg did not exactly allow for a creeping and stealthy gait.

It was more of a shuffle and clunk sort of gait.

Dainty and graceful, it was not.

Quiet, it was not.

Spy-like, it was not.

But it was the only gait she had, and surely she could not be as thunderous of foot as her ears told her she was at this moment. After all, no one came tearing out of rooms in fear of an imminent trampling when she walked during the day.

It was not only her own steps that she was painfully aware of, however. It was the knowledge that if she were in any way attacked, she would not be able to properly defend herself. If she heard sounds that indicated she ought to retreat, she would not be able to do so swiftly. If something were amiss in one of the darkened rooms she was passing, she was in no position to intervene.

She was not entirely powerless, of course. She was strong in body aside from her leg and had spent hours training at the Convent to ensure that her other limbs and her core were as taut and powerful as possible. Unfortunately, the altered gait of her right leg affected how her hips moved, which impacted how her back moved, which shifted how her shoulders moved, and…

Nothing in her body worked as it once did. She would never again be a fighter, or even a danger.

Just a cripple with the mind of a spy.

So she could only silently pray, while she shuffled down these hopefully empty halls and rooms, that Mr. Bichard was not hiding people in Coutanche House and that he himself was not a man of violence. Or nighttime wanderings.

Abby had good reason to suspect he did not do any such thing; she had spent the last three nights taking small ventures out of her room at various hours, and she had never met a single soul. She hadn't been as fearful in doing that as she was now, but there had been no danger on those walks. She had every possible excuse prepared, and all were perfectly reasonable.

Tonight, she had the same ones prepared, but she would be searching Mr. Bichard's study. Just a cursory examination at first, but after discussing some very basic details of the routines of the family with Mrs. Corbin, she had a few suspicions.

Mr. Bichard traveled rarely, but every other month or so, he did go away for a day or two to see to some investments. Mrs. Corbin was not certain as to his exact location for those ventures, but it was all fairly routine, and he was quick to return. Mr. Bichard was prone to Sunday walks among the caves, particularly in the early morning, which seemed odd, as the tide would surely still be in. And he received an inordinate amount of post and seemed to send out just as much.

Given there was not much to draw him away from his own home, Abby found the letters to be more suspicious than the Sunday morning walks. She had been under his employ for almost two weeks, and there had never been a single caller.

So how could he have such an extensive collection of letters coming in and out of this place? Who was writing to him? And to whom was he sending so many letters? And why, for heaven's sake, was this quiet, reclusive Frenchman involved in so much correspondence?

Some questions she might never fully answer, but she would settle for finding proof of his membership in the Faction, first of all.

Then, perhaps, some examination of the delivery of these letters and of what was sent out to note the patterns of such. And once she had that, she might be able to examine the contents. Or she could examine the contents first, if she wished. The breaking of seals and resealing them was really quite a simple matter, and one of the first areas in which she had been trained. But if there truly were as many letters as she had been led to believe, it would be a far better use of her time to open the letters that would actually prove useful rather than disrupt every single article of post Mr. Bichard had.

There would never be enough time for her to intercept every letter, read it, look for encryption, and reseal and send without someone noticing the delay. She had to be selective in her work in order to be in any way efficient.

And then there were those caves on his property… She could only hope that she'd kept her composure in front of him when she'd realized there were caves. The Faction regularly utilized caves on the shoreline in Kent, so why wouldn't they do the same here on Guernsey, on a known operative's property? But exploring those would take time and light, neither of which she had this evening.

Abby exhaled slowly, keeping her breath controlled and steady, ignoring the way her heart thundered and her throat tightened. She was moving about the house without a candle, which only made the space more imposing, but it also allowed her eyes to fully adjust to the darkness and see more detail without risking anyone else detecting her. And if the moon was high enough outside, she might be able to read anything she found by moonlight.

The study was soon before her, and she paused, closing her eyes and doing her best to force her mind and body to find the calm and intensity she had once known in moments like these. She might not be as physically capable anymore, but her mind was there, as was all of her training.

She could do this.

The door opened near silently, much to her relief, and the curtains were already drawn back, moonlight streaming in with utter brilliance. Her task would be much easier with that aid, and without having to disrupt the state of the room as it had been left. She took a moment to survey it as a whole.

Her tour of the house with the girls had been cursory at best, and there was never any reason for her to enter the master's study during the normal course of her day. The walls were lined with shelves, filled to the brim with books and trunks, as well as various items that must have been collected from travels, family heirlooms, or objects of fascination. The windows were massive, extending from floor to ceiling in a bay formation. The large, dark desk and chair faced away from the windows, but it was easy to imagine the figure of Mr. Bichard standing there, his back to the desk, staring out towards the sea.

Did these windows face France? Did he long for his life there as he had known it? What had brought him to Guernsey, and why did he remain?

That last question was a bit of a simple one, all things considered. His attachment to his wife was genuine, according to everyone Abby had spoken with, and she could easily imagine that he would not wish to be away from her final resting place.

Still, windows facing out towards the sea…

That was exactly how the windows of the Barcliffe library in Kent had been situated, which allowed the family to signal incoming ships transporting goods and operatives for the Faction. Was it possible that Bichard was doing the same here at Coutanche? There were no obvious signs of secret lower levels to the house where operatives could stay or goods could be stored…

But there were the caves.

Abby had yet to go to the spring to try and exercise in the warm water, but now she was even more interested in doing so. There were at least two other caves in close proximity to the one with the spring, and she could investigate those before getting into the water. But for now, she needed to see what this room could offer her.

She looked up at the ceiling, remembering the map that had been hidden in the artwork Sparrow had found at Barcliffe. But there was no artwork at all, only plaster detailing, and it was exactly the same across the entire room.

So much for similarities.

Abby began moving carefully along the outskirts of the room, her eyes tracing along each shelf as though she were looking for a book to read. She listened to the sound of the floorboards beneath her feet, examined the lines of the bookcases, eyed the differences in book heights and content—any detail that seemed out of place.

The shelves were clean, no hint of dust, which was unfortunate. She would know what was used most if the maids were not so diligent in their efforts, but she could manage. What was used most would be within sight and simple reaching distance, so if there was nothing unusual in the shelves or shocking in the books and items themselves…

Abby moved to the desk and sat in the chair, wincing as the leather groaned slightly with her pressure. But then it was silent, and she was able to look at the items that were the most convenient from this vantage point.

To her left, there was a shelf four down from the top, three from the bottom, that bore only books, all the same height, width, color. Even the binding seemed to be identical in this light.

To her right, the same shelf bore exactly the same sort of books, apart from one. One slightly taller, slightly thinner, slightly paler book. The only difference, suddenly glimmering to her eyes as though bathed in sunlight.

"There you are," Abby whispered with a quick grin. She pushed out of the chair and reached for the book, pulling it smoothly from the shelf and hefting it a little. Typical weight, so not a hollowed book…

She turned the book to open it, flipping through the pages quickly. A stray piece of paper within them caught her eye and she stopped, turning back to the spot.

It was folded in half, whatever it was, and she turned to the desk to lay the book flat. Taking another book from the desktop, she set it on the pages to hold them open. She would need to replace the paper exactly as she had found it, just in case the place was one of significance.

She slid the folded paper out of the pages and opened it, grinning at what was before her.

The music for *"Suspendez à ces murs."* The song used by the Faction to code their letters.

This was proof of Bichard's involvement.

She replaced the music in the book's pages, removing the other book from its surface, and began scanning through the other pages for hints. She came across a folded note in scribbled French with a date and time, but no other information of significance. The pages of the book spoke of the vanity of nobility and something about a detestable aristocracy, but certainly nothing about events, historical or otherwise. Nothing to shed further information on the date or time, even in vague tones.

Taking note of the page numbers, Abby replaced the folded scrap and continued to look through the pages. She found four other random bits of paper, each with small handwriting that only wrote out a word or two. A date or a phrase, but nothing that related to anything else as far as she could tell. She made sure everything was back in its place and turned to the first page, where the title was practically emblazoned.

An Essay on Privileges, and Particularly on Hereditary Nobility. Written by the Abbe Sieyès.

Abby's eyes widened as she stared at it.

Sieyès? The man who the Faction had been inspired by and held in such great esteem.

That was no coincidence.

Swallowing, she moved back to the shelf and replaced the book where she had found it, aligning everything perfectly so her involvement wouldn't be noticed.

She returned to the desk and sat once more, pulling at various drawers. A small ledger sat in one, and she flipped through it quickly. Everything was numbers, apart from the occasional circle and check mark in additional columns. No words at all, no descriptions. One column held numbers that were three digits long, another was two, and the third only one digit, and then came the two columns that were either blank, held a circle in the first, or a check in the second. There were only very rare occasions where there was a circle and a check.

None of that made any sense without context, which meant it was of no use at this moment.

But it would mean something eventually. No one kept ledgers like this without something to hide. Any other ledger would hold information, but this…

What was Bichard involved in?

Abby set the ledger back in its drawer and absently looked for something else, but came up empty-handed.

She walked about the room, looking every surface up and down. There were no hollow-sounding creaks from the floor, no other blatant items that did not belong, and no furniture that seemed out of place. There was the desk, the rug, the chair, the shelves, and a trunk. The trunk bore a sturdy lock, and she had not brought anything with which to pick it tonight.

So what happened in this room?

She began to pace, less for examination and more for thought. Whatever else he was to the Faction, Bichard was a devoted father, and he would never do something that would bring his daughters into harm's way. So if there were any involvement in bringing operatives through this house, they would never see the girls or come into the main of the house, which left only the caves, tunnels, and possibly a lower level of the house she had yet to see.

What was the date and location she had seen on that scrap of paper? She was not in a position to examine an atlas or diary at this moment, so that would need to wait for morning and a trip to the library. But the song was here, so he was certainly receiving coded messages.

The post would need to be intercepted. She'd known that already, but how could she possibly narrow down what she ought to look at? And how was she supposed to manage even doing so? What use would a governess have of the master's correspondence?

Abby rubbed at her brow, exhaling a short, irritated burst of air. It was going to be maddening to figure all of this out, and to try and do so before the Faction abducted another innocent girl and tried to marry her off to Bichard.

She shook her head, turning sharply on her heel. That did not—could not—make sense. Bichard rarely left Guernsey, and never associated with local Society, so why would he want to marry someone who could get him a position in London Society? Was there something to him that she just wasn't seeing? Was he really so devoted a soldier of the Faction?

Was he thinking of leaving Abby here with the girls while he had a new version of life in London with a bride of convenience and connection?

She shuddered at the idea. She might be a decent governess and have true affection for the girls, but she was not a replacement parent. The Gilles Bichard she had met would not want her to be, but was he the true version of the man or the carefully calculating Faction operative who could display whatever he liked?

His affection for his girls seemed genuine, and there was no denying their attachment to him. Children were not so easily trained and schooled in the arts of deception.

Well, Abby amended with a small smile, not typical children. There were plenty of children working with the various operatives who were geniuses at deception when they needed to be.

She looked around the study once more, searching for anything else that specifically drew her attention. She would be coming back to be more thorough in some of the less obvious places now that she had found what could be the beginning of a direction, and if Bichard happened to be out of the house for a decent amount of time, she could manage an examination in daylight as well.

But her priority would need to be the post and the caves for now.

Nodding once, Abby slipped back out into the corridor and made her way as softly as possible. She wasn't as concerned about being discovered now, but the way sounds were magnified in the middle of the night, especially when one wished for silence, was positively maddening. Especially knowing how silent she had once been.

It wouldn't do her any good to continually dwell on it, but there it was.

She did not take in a full breath until she was back in her room, the door safely shut and no sound of any disturbance from the corridor beyond it.

Then she exhaled with the entire weight of the world and sank onto her bed, letting her head drop with relief.

Her first return into the field, and she hadn't been caught, injured, or impeded.

That was a success, if nothing else was.

Craning her neck from side to side, she stood once more and

began preparing for bed, going over the details of her investigation, trying to make order of the random, hoping some connection might appear while she was focused on it. Once in her nightgown, she moved to her nightstand and pulled out her diary and a drawing pencil, recording all of the information she had found in the Sieyès book. One of the skills she often taught new recruits was that of improving memorization and recall through various techniques, but it had been some time since she'd had to employ them herself.

It was good to use those mental muscles once more.

She tapped her pencil against the nightstand in an absent pattern as she went over everything a final time. For whatever reason, she had thought the investigation here would be straightforward, if not outright simple. In her limited physical condition, why shouldn't it have been something rather rudimentary?

Foolish, idiotic notion. As if Milliner would have pulled her out of the school and back into the field for something a trainee could have done.

No, this was going to be complicated and messy and incredibly detailed, whatever it was.

"They don't assign missions out of pity, Abigail," she scolded herself harshly under her breath.

Had that been lurking in the back of her mind all this time? That they were giving her this assignment, making it sound important and that she was perfect for it, when it wasn't but wanting to make her feel useful? How long had she worked with these individuals and organizations? She knew that wasn't how anything worked, especially where lives and security of the kingdom was concerned. They took no chances, and only those properly equipped for a situation were sent.

If she was here, it was because she was capable of accomplishing the required task, and as a longstanding operative, asset, and instructor, she had developed skills that not all spies could boast.

She could do this in a very particular way, unique to her skills and personality.

"And you would tell your trainees and students the very same," she insisted aloud.

That made her smile just a little. She would have said a great deal more to students and trainees, been very encouraging, and known exactly what to say to soothe their nerves and prepare their minds.

So why did that not work for herself?

Time to retrain herself, it seemed.

Pearl needed to meet Sage and learn from her. And then Pearl could adapt and grow in her own right.

The sooner, the better.

Chapter Eight

Gilles shook his head as he read his most recent letter of instructions from his Faction handler. It was the same sort of nonsense he had been asked to do over and over again, without much variation. Take the letters he received, change the seal to one with the crest he'd been given when he joined the Faction, and send them on to a contact in England, who would see them distributed to all the intended Faction members. It allowed them to send messages from France to England with more secrecy and security, but it was such a hassle, and more than half of the information in the letters was speculative now.

Of course, Gilles did the same thing for letters coming from supporters in England to the Faction in France. Those were usually more interesting, and allowed him to take better stock of the situation brewing there. That was when he could take up what Heloise had begun and relay information to his British contacts.

He loved doing that. He almost never had proof that his tips were successful, but occasionally, Trick or Trace or Briar would inform him. More often than not, though, they had messages sent to him asking for specific information on a person or situation arising in their particular sector of the London docks.

They never messaged him directly, of course. Their information went to a man in a pub in Poplar, and he received it from a ship captain whom Gilles trusted implicitly. The man did not know Gilles's name, but he knew where his loyalty lay. He knew Gilles was called Briton to those in England who knew of him, and that was enough. Gilles had loved when Heloise had coined that name for them. It played on Gilles's home province of Brittany, a place he would always adore but might never reside in again.

Perhaps one day…

The man who delivered Faction mail had no idea what he was delivering, so he had no need to care about loyalty, alliances, or the like. He only wanted his fees for doing the thing, which were handsomely paid on both sides.

The lovely thing about living on Guernsey was that people were neither French nor English, and yet somehow both. Not in all ways, but certainly in some. So whatever the Faction wanted to do left Guernsey and the other Channel Islands alone for the most part. And since England did not want to get too close to France, they felt the same. Perhaps it would serve England to have one of their officially trained operatives here, but until Gilles was involved in actual discussions with those who made such decisions, he would keep that opinion to himself.

Gilles sighed as he looked down at his letter now, shaking his head again. He didn't even have letters from the Faction to send on right now, just this note for him alone. He operated under the assumption that unless his instructions changed, he was to keep acting as he was and forwarding letters accordingly. The constant reminders to keep working for the cause were utterly pointless and a waste of parchment.

But what did he know? He could only glean information from the letters he received and try to piece things together.

Heloise would have had some creative and derogatory remark for this note. She always did and had always managed to turn Gilles's annoyance to humor.

There was no pain with remembering this about her—only fondness and a little sadness to color it differently.

That was progress, surely.

Shoving the letter into his desk, Gilles rose and glanced out of the window, noting the downpour of rain. There would be no beach outing today, then. The girls and Abigail would be in the house.

He smiled at the idea and rapped his knuckles on the desk surface as he rounded it, leaving the room in search of them.

It took some time to locate the trio, as they were not in the nursery, schoolroom, or kitchens. He found them in the library, of all places, each with a large tome of literature on their laps.

He folded his arms and leaned against the doorjamb with a curious smile. "What in the world is going on in here?"

All three looked up at him with grins. "Atlases, sir," Abigail chirped with as much eagerness as a child. "We are exploring the world."

Gilles tilted his head, his smile growing. "I have three atlases?"

"You do," she confirmed, returning to her own. "Different years of publication, but three all the same."

"How excessive of me." He pushed into the room and sat on the floor in front of his girls. "And what are we exploring today? Ah, South America. Mariette, would you like to see such a place?"

She shook her head very firmly. "Too far," she said simply.

He grinned and ruffled her beautiful curls. *"Oui, c'est vrai, ma chérie.* You'd better stay here with Papa. And you, Madeline? Where have you gone today?"

"Belgium, Papa!" She showed him the map on her page. "Is that too far from us?"

"Non, ma chérie, that is not far at all." He tapped her cheek with a gentle finger. "I have been to Belgium before."

The girls looked at him with gaping mouths. "You have?" Madeline asked in a hushed voice.

Chuckling, Gilles traced his finger around the map of Belgium until he found Brussels. *'Oui.* When I was a boy, my parents took my brother and me there for a summer. It was a marvelous place, especially for boys who had rarely left Quimper. Even Paris could not compare for me then. I'd seen Paris a few times when we visited my aunt, and so it was no longer exciting. Brussels, though, was an adventure."

"I want an adventure," Madeline said with pure longing as she looked at the map again.

Gilles glanced at Abigail, noting the suspicious tension at the corners of her lips and the lines forming at her eyes. Her eyes flicked to his, and he caught the mirth within them, echoing his own that was steadily growing in his chest.

"You have plenty of adventures, *ma fée,*" Gilles assured Madeline. "Hasn't Mademoiselle Chorley taught you about your imagination yet?"

Madeline's head bobbed in a series of nods. "But I want a real adventure, Papa. Somewhere that isn't Guernsey."

That was fair, and Gilles couldn't pretend otherwise. His daughters had never left the island, and he'd never been particularly inclined to take them anywhere. He and Heloise had discussed visiting France as a family one day, but until the Faction was either eliminated or under control, they hadn't wanted to take the risk of entering the country. England was almost as dangerous, considering the game he was playing. Risking his daughters was not something he was willing to do, but he did not want them to lead secluded lives either.

He would lose them to adulthood one day, but he wanted to keep them his precious little ones as long as he could.

"Someday, we will get you a real adventure or two," he relented with a heavy sigh, smiling down at his oldest and stroking her cheek. "I promise. You just need to be a little bit older."

Madeline made a face at him, then giggled as she went back to her atlas.

Gilles looked at Abigail again. "And where has Mademoiselle Chorley decided to go for her atlas adventure?"

She turned the book to show him. "Australia, sir."

He raised a brow at her. "Do you have some criminals you wish to visit? Or some you wish to send off?"

Abigail laughed easily, the sound catching him in the chest just as it had done that day he'd shown her the caves. "No, I've simply always been curious about it. So far away, so different from England, but part of the kingdom. I would say that I'd love to see it myself, but I think a journey on the sea that long would be a very slow, excruciating death for me."

Gilles tsked softly, fighting further laughter. "So no far-off adventures for Mademoiselle Chorley either. My, my, what are we going to do about this?" He put his chin in his hand and frowned darkly, pretending to think hard.

The girls watched him, both frowning exactly as Heloise used to when she was thinking.

It was a pleasant reminder that she would never be fully removed from his life.

"How can we take far-off adventures without having to board a ship?" Gilles asked, as though it were a troublesome puzzle he could not solve.

Madeline gasped and raised her hand high as though in a schoolroom.

Hiding a smile, Gilles looked directly at her. "Yes, Madeline? You have an idea?"

She nodded eagerly, her hand returning to her lap. "We can read books, Papa. Maman always said that stories are adventures for our minds and imagination, sometimes even better than playing."

"C'est vrai, ma chérie," he praised, smiling fully. "She loved books very much."

"Mademoiselle Abby likes books, too," Marie-Claire added quickly. "She's going to start reading to us before bed."

"Is she?" Gilles looked at Abigail with interest, something warm and ticklish unfurling in the pit of his stomach.

Abigail nodded without reservation. "I could get lost in books for weeks on end. It was one of the few things in my life that did not change in the least after my injury. Books saved my sanity during recovery."

Gilles softened at that, his warmth spreading from shoulder to shoulder and down to the tips of his fingers. He couldn't help the smile he sent her way, knowing it was gentle and tender and probably far too familiar, but not caring. Abigail needed to know that she had his sympathy, his understanding, his support. She also needed to know that he was not only her employer, but her friend. At least, he would be if she would let him.

She needed to stop calling him Mr. Bichard or sir. He wanted her to call him by his name, and he wanted her to take her meals with him. He wanted her to come to the library after the girls were asleep so the two of them could discuss their favorite books. He wanted to go for a stroll in the gardens with her and discover her favorite flower. He wanted her to go to the pool in the cave and try exercising in the warm water and then come back and tell him if it worked. He wanted to help her get stronger and more flexible, if there was even the slightest possibility. He wanted to dance with her at a ball.

He hadn't wanted to even attend a ball since Heloise had died. He'd never really wanted to go when she was alive, but he endured it for her because he loved dancing with her. Only her.

And now he wanted to dance with Abigail.

And from what she had told him, she could not even dance.

He didn't care. They could dance in the privacy of this house, away from other dancers, any finery, and even musicians to serenade them.

He just wanted to have her in his arms.

His throat tightened and he felt his eyes widen as the desires and ideas he now had raced upon him with a vengeance. He lowered his gaze to the rug to keep from showing anything to Abigail or the girls. It was too much too soon, and not well-defined. It was just… it was only…

He hadn't wanted anything of the sort in so long, and now suddenly his heart was breaking free of its cage and being lit on fire.

How was *that* for a revelation?

"*Zut,*" he whispered to himself, shaking his head. He cleared his throat and forced a smile on his face as he raised his head, looking at the girls in particular. "Would you like to hear my favorite story I've found in books?"

"Yes, Papa!" they cheered, setting their atlases aside and scooting closer to him.

His eyes slid to Abigail just enough to see her tilt her head in curiosity as she set her own atlas aside.

Good. He wanted her to hear this as well.

"A long, long time ago," Gilles began, lowering his voice dramatically, "there was a soldier named Odysseus, King of Ithaca. He had been fighting in the Trojan War for ten years, but he was now trapped on the island of Ogygia when he just wanted to go home."

"How did he get trapped?" Marie-Claire asked in a loud whisper, her eyes round.

Gilles gave her a very serious look. "We don't know. Odysseus hasn't told us that yet."

Her mouth formed an O, and she said nothing else, watching

him.

He nodded at her attention. "But he is being kept on this island because he has angered Poseidon, god of the seas."

"How?" Marie-Claire gasped, her hands flying to her cheeks.

Annoyance and amusement rose together on a gentle wave within him as he gave his daughter an exasperated look. "We don't know yet, *petite*."

She nodded slowly, still gaping, as though in a trance.

"Back at his home in Ithaca, Odysseus's son, Telemachus, lives with his mother, Penelope. And there are many young men who want to marry Penelope, as they believe Odysseus is dead."

Gilles continued to tell them the very beginnings of *The Odyssey*, keeping everything at an appropriate level for children of their age. Given the sheer volume of the epic poem, there was no way he would be able to tell them the entire story in one sitting, but he didn't mind that. It had been some time since he had shared a story with his girls, and if he could extend their desire for such a thing for a few days or weeks by sharing his favorite story, he would gladly take it.

He only got the story to the end of perhaps the fourth book or so by the time they were interrupted by Mrs. Corbin about the usual teatime for the girls.

Madeline and Marie-Claire groaned at being interrupted. "Mrs. Corbin!" Madeline scolded, propping her hands on her hips much like the housekeeper did on a regular basis. "Not yet! We need to get back to Odysseus on the island! Telemachus is going to find him!"

Mrs. Corbin blinked at the girls, then looked at Gilles in utter bewilderment. "What in the name of St. Sampson is she talking about?"

Gilles barked a loud laugh at the invocation of the patron saint of Guernsey. "I was telling them my favorite story, Mrs. Corbin. *The Odyssey*."

She only stared at him. "The odyssey of what?"

Abigail snorted a very soft laugh before coughing to cover it up, looking down at the rug beneath them with great interest.

Gilles was no less amused, but contained it well. "*The Odyssey*, Mrs. Corbin. The original epic poem from Ancient Greece. Written by Homer, most likely. Trojan War. Greek gods. Family. Battles.

Desperate suitors who meet an untimely end out of vengeance."

There wasn't a scintilla of recognition in her eyes, and Gilles clamped down on his lips hard to keep from laughing further.

Mrs. Corbin exhaled shortly. "And that is your favorite story?" She shook her head at his nod. "We need to have you read a wider variety of books, sir. Come along, girls. Cook has made several new biscuits for you to try. You may hear more of the story later, if you wish."

Grumbling but obedient, the girls rose and gave Gilles quick hugs before following her out of the library for their tea.

Only when they were gone did Gilles and Abigail look at each other, exploding into roaring laughter almost at once. Abigail's warm, throaty laughter echoed all around them, her eyes squeezed tightly shut with mirth, one arm going around her stomach as though trying to protect her ribs from the laughter. Her cheeks grew flushed the more she laughed, and just as before, her throat danced with the sounds.

Gilles could barely catch his breath for his own laughter, but when combined with the stirring sight that was Abigail's amusement, he was finding air in short supply, making his own laughter sound like wheezing. Which, of course, was even more hilarious than anything else already was.

Neither of them could stop for the longest time, and tears were streaming from both of their eyes before long.

Abigail wiped at hers, still giggling breathlessly. "Oh, that was too perfect. Her face!" She tried to recreate the unimpressed, confused expression Mrs. Corbin had worn, but there was too much mirth in her face to manage anything convincing. She dissolved into giggles again, leaning back on both hands and trying to steady her breathing.

Gilles brushed his sleeve along his cheeks, exhaling slowly in his own attempt to soothe the hilarity. "I had no idea that my taste in reading would be such a disappointment."

"She didn't even know what you were talking about," Abigail scoffed with another bright laugh. "Not that I can blame her. Many people don't know *The Odyssey* unless they've been fortunate enough to have tutors who enjoy it, and outside of the upper classes, who would even have the opportunity?"

That was true, and something Gilles had never truly considered before this moment. He had taken so many things for granted in his life, especially with the station he was born into and the fortune he'd inherited. He tried not to live his life wearing the same blinders that others did. But, it seemed, he had not quite succeeded there. He had presumed his housekeeper would know *The Odyssey* without considering anything else.

He didn't feel guilt over that, exactly. Gilles was quite certain Mrs. Corbin knew plenty of stories that he did not, and perhaps someday they could share them with each other. It could create a more level education and imagination for them both.

Chuckling, Gilles stretched out his legs and leaned back on his elbows. "Perhaps I ought to invite her to listen to the story with the girls. She might find a new favorite story for herself."

Abigail laughed softly, almost to herself. "Somehow, I doubt it. She would heartily disapprove of Calypso keeping him captive and falling in love with him while he is her prisoner. Who knows what she would make of Circe seducing his men?"

Gilles looked at her in surprise, not bothering to hide his delight at her knowledge. "Ah, so you know the story, then."

"I do," Abigail replied simply, her smile wide. At his questioning look, she laughed once and shrugged. "I have siblings, we've discussed that before. Our family's library contained several books intended for my brothers' education. I have always been a voracious reader, so I read everything in there. Including *The Odyssey* and *The Iliad*."

"You ready *everything* in there?" Gilles asked with some suspicion, teasing entering his voice without any real intention.

Abigail rolled her eyes, her lips curving to one side in a wry grin. "Fine, I started to read every book in there, but did not finish them all. It is not entirely my fault; I don't think anyone has ever read *A Dedicated History of the Livestock Farming of Shropshire* from cover to cover. And I am sorry to the author, but *A Treatise on the Application and Understanding of Greek Philosophies on Birds* was intolerable. I could not read beyond the second chapter; it was too abysmal a prospect."

Gilles was back to laughing without realizing it at first, and

Abigail soon joined him again.

"But," she managed when her laughter faded, "I did enjoy *The Odyssey*. I did always wonder about the sheep, though. How in the world could grown men hide on the underbellies of sheep? I have seen many, many flocks in my life, and not one of the sheep in a single flock could actually hide a man, let alone carry one."

"Polyphemus was blind by that point!" Gilles cried out, still laughing. "Odysseus and the men were hiding their footsteps."

Abigail turned to face him, her expression incredulous. "That is one point for them, but it does not address how the sheep managed to actually carry a single man! It's a sheep, not a cow."

It was impossible to avoid smiling at this woman sitting on the floor of his library and debating *The Odyssey* with him so vehemently. *He wanted…*

"Perhaps the sheep in the twelfth century were larger," Gilles began seriously, forcing his smile to fade. "I wonder if completing your reading of that livestock farming book would have given you insight there, but *hélas,* we will never know now."

Abigail's eyes went wide for a moment before a rather indelicate and drawn-out snort escaped her. One hand clapped over her mouth as her eyes scrunched shut with silent laughter.

Gilles heaved a dramatic sigh. "Quite a lesson we have learned today, would you not agree, Mademoiselle Governess? One must always complete one's reading."

Her laughter could not be contained by her hand now, and she fell back onto one elbow, her delight and amusement on full display. *He wanted.*

Gilles shook his head, letting himself give in to more laughter as his head swam with the wonderment of his feelings.

"Would you like to join us for more stories from *The Odyssey,* Abigail?" he asked softly as his laughter eased.

She beamed, still wreathed in mirth. "Of course, sir."

"Gilles," he corrected quickly. At her surprised look, he shrugged. "When we're like this, can I not be Gilles?"

"I don't… know…" she murmured, tilting her head a little, her eyes surveying him with a light he could not interpret.

He swallowed the temptation to close the distance between them and kiss her, looking away. "Just consider it, Abigail. I think I'd like to be Gilles to you from time to time."

Abigail made no response for so long, he wondered if he might have offended her. But then, so softly he almost missed it, she replied, "All right."

Chapter Nine

The new path Mr. Bichard had shown her to use for the beach was a much easier one for Abby to traverse, and there was no mistaking it. The ground was more level, the descent more gradual, and the distance to the bottom shorter, all of which meant it was perfect for her. It was a bit farther away from the house than the path she had taken the first time she'd gone to the water, but far more suited to her condition and far less likely to leave her sore and more unsteady later.

It was a gorgeous day, and she couldn't help but tilt her head back and inhale the fresh sea air deeply before exhaling a peaceful sigh. She was free to spend as much time as she wished down here this morning, and she was going to take full advantage of it.

Not just for her leg, but for her assignment as well.

She was wearing a plain morning dress at the moment, with a sturdy set of stays and a chemise beneath, and the plan was for her to slip the outer dress and stays off and step into the pool in the chemise. Mrs. Corbin had assured her that the caves were private property, and no one would trespass, so she could have bathed "naturally," as the housekeeper had put it, but there was nothing appealing about being naked in a cave. A cold, dark, dank cave beneath the estate of her employer.

She was vulnerable enough as it was, but that…

She shivered at the very idea.

And the water would make everything even colder, her shiver reminded her.

But before she did any of that, she had some investigating to do.

There was no such thing as making haste with her gait, but she did try to quicken her pace and lengthen her stride. The sooner she looked at the caves, the sooner she could be in the warm pool doing some exercises.

She was not naive enough to expect much of a difference to her leg even with the warm water, but she could honestly say it was something she had not tried. And she had determined long ago that she would try everything she could to heal and improve. Any chance to possibly get her old body back. Her old flexibility. Her old maneuverability.

Any maneuverability.

Any at all.

If she could be any less of a cripple, she would try.

She reached the caves just a few moments later and passed the first one, remembering that was where the warm pool was. The second cave was smaller than the first, narrower as well as shorter, and it seemed to funnel down far more quickly. Still, Abby looked over every inch of it she could see as she wandered in, and soon enough found the very back of the cave without any secrets, tunnels, or clues. So if there was anything to this place, it would only be a superficial meeting place or a nook to hide from storms. Nothing more than that, which meant she could move on.

Elimination was almost as delightful as success, in this case.

Keeping each step careful and attentive, Abby made her way back to the cave entrance, squinting at the bright sunshine as she emerged back out onto the beach. The water reached a little closer to the third cave than the other two, even at this time of day when the tide was out, so she kept her steps as close to the stone as possible. It made those steps even more tremulous than usual, but water would far and away be worse.

The third cave was absolutely monstrous compared to the other two. From the width of its opening to the height of its expanse to the complete lack of a back wall that the eye could see, it might have been the mouth of some dreadful and long-perished sea creature. It could have fit an entire ship within its depths, at least in some places. Perhaps not one of the grander ships of the line, and perhaps not all of the masts and sails, but enough of one, nevertheless.

Abby shook her head as she ventured in. This one would take longer to explore, given its size. And its depth, if the lack of rear wall was any indication. She'd need a torch when she reached a certain point, and that would make things difficult. But she would do her best as it was and see what she noticed.

Small divots in the rocky floor beneath her feet indicated years of dripping water from above, and the larger craters of sorts still held water from the nightly floodings. Her first inspection was of the ground itself, as Sparrow had found a button of a Faction operative in a cave on the Kent coastline last year. Abby wasn't expecting such luck herself, but she would never forgive herself if she didn't make certain the same thing was not found here. The problem would be the sheer size of this cave and the amount of ground she would need to inspect, not to mention the darkness that increased the farther she ventured.

But if she could come here just after dawn, she might be able to get some direct sunlight into this cave and reach its very farthest possible distance. It might not give her much more than broad daylight, but it would not hurt anything to try.

She frowned to herself as she continued into the cave, not seeing anything of note on the ground, nor along the walls beside her. But the dimensions were shrinking, bit by bit in all directions, the deeper she went, so there was some narrowing to consider. A strange nook of sorts seemed to be carved out to her right, and four fishing boats sat together, neatly lined up with a pair of oars for each.

That could be considered unusual, but also could be easily explained away by locals using the cave and cove for fishing. It was much the same in Kent, in Cornwall, and probably several other counties as well, so why should Guernsey be any different? But they were situated fairly far back into the cave, all things considered. Why not keep them closer to the entrance? Still, she would not pretend to understand such things, and there was no sense in applying significance where none ought to be.

She moved past the boats deeper into the cave, the light beginning to fade at this point, but her eyes were adjusting to the change in time with her paces, so she was not overly concerned as yet. The ground still contained the damp divots, but it also contained small hills of sorts, making the surface even more perilous for her. Much like walking on ice, in her mind.

Why was the footwear for women so useless for any surface other than perfectly flat and gently textured?

The sound of the waves outside was echoing within the cave, but it was growing more distant as well. She could hear the ominous dripping sounds from deeper within, and that was growing louder still. It wasn't a pattering sort of sound, as though multiple points were producing these droplets, but perhaps three all told, apart from the echoes that they produced. One of them was hitting water, but the other two just hit the ground itself. But how far into the cave were these droplets? It sounded close, but she wasn't seeing anything that could make those sounds at that volume.

There had to be some sort of widening deeper into the cave, a sort of room that had formed and encased the space to create its own echo chamber of sorts.

But she wasn't seeing it yet. That was peculiar.

The cave continued to narrow in all directions, now rather steeply and sharply, and soon she would have to climb. She could not do so here and now, especially without knowing how far back this would go and how long it would take to explore. There were no obvious signs of anything Faction related, but what was obvious and what was Faction related? What was she even looking for? This cave was easily accessible by walking and by the sea, and extended far enough back to be used in many ways, and that was all she could say.

Further investigation was required, but it would serve much better to be done by someone who wouldn't injure themselves just by walking on this surface.

As though her thoughts could curse her actions, Abby felt her feet give way against the slick ground. Her knees hit the ground hard, her right harder than her left, and her hands scraped against the rocks in an attempt to catch herself. She could feel the skin breaking against the scattered pebbles dotting the ground, her nails scraping against the damp rock in a futile attempt to find purchase. Her face avoided any damage, but she certainly felt the air vanish from her lungs with the impact.

She lay there on her stomach a moment, closing her eyes and

praying she was not actually injured beyond her own mobility. If she did not move, nothing hurt excessively.

Aside from her palms, which burned where they'd been scratched. Alas for the delicate, soft hands of elegant females.

Not that Abby fell into that category.

She turned, shifting her legs to their sides and pushing herself up to a sitting position. Her wrists and hands screamed against any surface, so she did her best not to press them much, but there was no way she could stand without their use. And her bad knee was definitely going to be worse than usual, but the warm springs were next on her list, so perhaps she could soothe these pains before they became too great.

Abby clamped down on her lips hard, knowing the pain that was about to come and willing her body to find the strength to get through it. She exhaled slowly, then took in another breath and exhaled once more. Then she placed her palms flat on the ground before her and pushed up to her knees, biting back whimpers and pants of pain. Tucking her toes against the ground, she pushed up again from her knees to her feet, her breath catching in agony at the sharp stings racing along both legs and hands.

But then she was upright, and she turned back for the entrance to the cave, her legs shaking and her gait even more shuffling than her usual limp made it. She all but clung to the wall for balance and stability as she moved, her teeth grinding against each other as her pain increased with every step. There was no relief in movement, but pain was relative. She had endured worse, and she could endure this. It did not matter that pain was her constant companion; her nerves were so attuned to any new pain that she seemed to feel it tenfold.

She had rarely noticed pain before her injury. But now…

She shook her head, determined to keep herself from dwelling on that. She'd suffered a fall, and that was all. She would be sore, but no true damage would be done. Her hands were cut, her fingers were dirty, her nails uneven, but there was no true harm done. Self-pity and dramatics could not have place here. She would be no good to Milliner if she simpered about something as trivial as this.

Step by trembling step, Abby eventually reached the cave opening and sighed in relief. The rocky ground of the shore itself was much easier than the slick surface of the caves, and she would have a few moments of relative steadiness until she went into the first cave for the warm pool. She was tempted to take her time to do so, but time was not her friend in this.

She did, however, move to the shore first and place her hands into the gentle waters that lapped against the pebbles at her feet. The stinging eased in the frigid water, and she brushed as much of the rocky debris from her palms and fingers as she could. The cuts and scrapes would heal on their own, and there was very little blood there, but she would certainly be tender for a time. She hadn't even thought about wearing any sort of outdoor gloves for this venture. Might that have protected her at all?

There was no way to tell, and she could only release a short sigh of inevitability at the situation.

Her hands now cleaner and the pain of them more frozen, she hobbled towards the first cave, her injured leg already stiffening and practically dragging behind her. She carefully inched within the cave, her fingertips gripping at the walls to help steady her walking. She wouldn't find anything to latch on to, but at least she could use it for balance.

And she was going to be even more cautious with her steps, given the terrain and her lack of ability to successfully navigate it today. Her fresh injuries would only make that worse, and a second set of injuries would be disastrous.

Abby shook her head at herself hard as she neared the warm pool. There was nothing she hated more than the weakness she had gained these last five years. She could train as much as she wanted in other respects, but having a crippled body would mean she'd never be wholly strong again. Only partially. Only specifically.

Only incompletely.

She released a sigh of relief as she reached the pool without stumbling, slipping, or crashing to the ground again. She walked around to the spot where Mr. Bichard—*Gilles*—had indicated ease of entry and gingerly let herself sink to the ground. She removed her shoes and stockings, followed by her dress and her stays, folding everything and putting them into a tidy pile a safe distance from the edge of the pool.

Scooting to the edge of the water, Abby dipped one foot into the pool, smiling to herself at the warm temperature. It was not as warm as the baths she enjoyed from time to time, but it was certainly warmer than any seawater she had ever encountered. She slid down into the water as gently as possible, her legs protesting the change in their bruised state, but then gasped as the slight chill of being in water ricocheted over her body in a series of gooseflesh.

But it was soon gone, and after paddling around the pool for a moment or two, she was perfectly adjusted to the water. She swam over to one of the edges and placed her back against it, her toes touching the bottom while the water lapped about her shoulders.

Then she frowned.

How, exactly, was she supposed to exercise her leg? She'd never done anything like this with a doctor or with Fists or Morna at the school, and even in her recovery right after her accident, there had never been any specific work done with her leg. If there had been… if someone had known a little more and given her just that much guidance…

Would it have made a difference? Could it have?

Abby cocked her head to one side, biting her lip. She raised her bad leg in the water, just directly in front of her at first, and then swung it from side to side. There was a twinge of pain when she went all the way out to her side with it, but directly at her hip. That was strange, she had never noticed specific pain in her hip from motion. Only ever the aching at the end of a day when she had done too much.

Interesting.

She brought her leg back in front of her, then began to bend her knee.

A sharp yelp ripped from her throat at the searing pain her knee sent up and down her entire leg with the motion. She hissed softly as she tried again with less intensity and found the pain more manageable. Not gone by a long shot—her fall earlier would make certain of that—but manageable. She straightened her leg in the same steady, careful motion, then repeated the action twice more, grinning to herself when the last one barely hurt at all.

Then she moved her leg out at a new angle from her body and worked on bending and straightening again. Minimal discomfort, no pain.

She squealed in private delight and tried to bend her knee further than before, and found the motion there, to her amazement. She hadn't really tried to bend her knee very far in a way she could notice for the last several years, so she had no idea if this was better or worse than before. She simply used her leg as it allowed and went on with life.

What if she had been doing this all along? She would know exactly where she had started and how far she had to go. But that was no matter; she could start now and improve with time.

Abby worked her leg, her knee, her ankle, her very toes in every direction she could think of, with every motion physically possible. Anything that was within the capabilities of her scarred and withered leg, she tried. She pushed hard through the rising discomfort to the point of the pain she had felt when she'd first started.

It felt so amazing to move like this. Even with the pain, it was the most brilliant feeling in the world. Her leg felt more alive and alert than it had in the last five years, and the work she had been doing seemed to get better and better with each motion. She felt stronger than she had in any recent memory.

Well, that wasn't precisely true, but her muscles positively throbbed up and down her right leg, and not in a painful way. In a good way. In a delicious way.

In a *strong* way.

She was going to do it. She was going to get all of the motion and strength back in her leg. She wasn't going to be crippled forever, and she would be able to do all of the things she had missed. She would ride and run and dance and…

It would take months. Months and months, and many hours of doing these exercises, until she had all of the motion possible. Then it would be strength she sought. Strength she could build up, and she would find a way to make it all possible. She could see it all before her now, perfectly reflected in her mind's eye. She saw herself returning to the training grounds at the Convent, fully dressed in the tunics they all wore for fight exercises, twirling a staff as she prepared to enter the ring. She faced every operative in hand-to-hand combat, her legs flying with kicks and blows that would make the male operatives jealous. She ran the obstacle course on the grounds with glorious ease, even as her brow glinted with the sheen of healthy perspiration. She was back within the ranks of operatives, racing through the dark with Ivy on one side and Iris on the other, silencing guards and retrieving information, vanishing from fortresses without a trace.

Exhilaration unlike anything Abby had ever known raced over her, and she sighed at the glow that seemed to fill her heart and mind. She was going to positively float back to Coutanche House at this rate, and she'd probably wear a dreamy smile the entire afternoon and evening. And she would have to find an exquisite gift for Gilles for opening this door for her.

Her bliss shattered as she recollected just who Gilles Bichard was and what she was doing here in the first place.

This man—this Faction member—was giving her the way to reclaim her operative status while he was actively trying to bring down everything she stood for. He was the enemy, not the hero. He was part of the problem, not the solution. He had no idea who she was, let alone who she had been, and she could use his apparent kindness against him one day, but she would not be showering him with any sort of gratitude. He was one of them. Once she got her strength and agility back, she would be actively dismantling the thing he held only less precious than his daughters.

The thought of the girls broke through her ire like a sabre and Abby dropped her head and her leg. He adored those girls, and if she actually did anything to destroy their lives… She couldn't do it. Couldn't rid them of a father when they'd already lost their mother.

No, the Bichards would have to remain untouched physically. The Faction would be destroyed, but not the Bichards.

She could help with that. Perhaps put in a word for them when they inevitably brought down the Faction and made everyone involved from England pay for their crimes. She could find a way to keep the girls with their father and allow them some sort of normal childhood. It would be the best for everyone, surely.

Biting her lip as she thought of options, Abby started towards the slant of the pool again, this time to make her exit. She used her arms and her stronger left leg to get purchase on the ground and hauled herself out of the pool. Her knee still shot flashes of pain down her leg from the fall earlier, but she could deal with that while she got out.

She moved to the pile of clothing she'd folded earlier, wishing she'd brought some linen or toweling to dry off, but she hadn't thought of that when she'd come. After all, that was part of what the thicker morning dress was for. A breeze from the sea whipped into the cave and chilled her soaked frame in a single ripple, and she gasped out a shiver.

Her stays went back on first, shielding at least that part of her from the coldest part of the breeze. She started putting on her dress, standing to manage it better, when her right knee completely buckled beneath her, sending her not only to the ground, but back into the warm pool with a vengeance. There was instantaneous burning in both knees and shins, as though the fall had sliced her legs open afresh and the warm mineral water was searing the exposed flesh. Abby shrieked as her face broke the surface of the water, every good feeling from before eviscerated in a moment only made possible by her injury. Her stupid, crippling, life-altering injury.

She wasn't going to get her operative standing back. Her imagination had strayed too far before, and she needed to rein herself back in. The most she could hope for was a diminished limp and a return to more able-bodied activities. And if she had just done herself more of an injury than her previous fall, she would not be anywhere close to where she had been when she woke up this morning.

She swallowed back a hot wash of frustrated, heartbroken tears as she made her way back to the slight embankment, struggling to even get her good knee on the ground. But thanks to whatever strength remained in her arms, she managed to get back out of the water and onto the damp rock, panting hard at the ridiculous exertion required of her.

Failure.

That was the only word she could use at this moment.

She was a failure. Her assignment would be a failure. Her injury had made her career a failure. And she would probably be a failure at being a governess for these sweet Bichard girls because she was so desperate to get herself back into some sort of impressive graces with the Shopkeepers that she would ruin their father needlessly.

A man who had never done her any personal harm. Who laughed with her over *The Odyssey*. Who told her about warm pools to strengthen and work her weak leg. Who watched her walk down the path to the shore to make sure she didn't fall.

Whose eyes crinkled when he smiled.

A man whom she genuinely liked and found particularly handsome. Especially when he smiled at her. And when he laughed. And when he called her Abigail.

But not just any man. Gilles Bichard. Gilles…

Damn.

Now her assignment was destined to fail. She could not have tender feelings about her target, and yet here she was. Lying weakly on damp rock in a cave beneath his property and feeling warm and restless at the thought of him.

Perhaps she ought to fling herself back into the pool a third time for good measure and see if some of the sense she had lost might return to her.

But she did not trust her body to get her out of the pool a third time, so she only pulled herself farther from the water and tried to crawl without using her bruised and likely bleeding legs. It was an awkward series of movements to do so, but she couldn't bring herself to try the use of her knees in such a way again. Not right now. Not when letting them rest and recover felt so much better.

Her dress was only half on, now dripping wet with the rest of her, but it was utterly ruined from the fall and from her now dragging herself along the cave floor. It might protect her modesty, but not much else. It certainly hadn't protected her body when she fell.

This entire venture was foolish. Why was she even trying?

She finally got to the wall and turned over, using her arms to force herself into a seated position and pressing her back against it. Only then did she glance down at her legs.

Blood inched its way down both legs, cuts on her knees and shins adding to the slow-moving stream as it trickled along. It would become more of a raging river when she stood, though it was hardly disastrous. Only uncomfortable, unsightly, and inconvenient.

There was no point in putting on her stockings when she was

bleeding like this, unless she truly wished to ruin them, but she did replace her shoes, though she was not certain how well they would work if she continued to bleed as she was. There was something rather distasteful about the idea of walking in puddles of her own blood.

If she could hurry home, it would be fine.

Her shoes on, Abby placed her feet flat on the ground and gripped at the wall behind her, shoving herself up to standing. She wobbled a moment, steadied, then took a step.

She crumpled in a pile of weakness and pain at once, but caught herself before any more injury could take place. Her knee had completely buckled, unable to hold her up at all. And her good leg refused to compensate, it seemed.

Right, then. She would have to pull herself out of this cave and to the house by her arms or try and hop on one leg.

Or a combination of both.

Tears sprang to her eyes as she began to use her arms and hands to move towards the cave entrance. Tears of frustration, embarrassment, and pain. Tears of defeat and hopelessness. Tears of dashed hopes and dreams, even more crushing for not having had hopes and dreams for years.

Tears for the sake of tears alone.

Chapter Ten

Gilles tore from the house at a breakneck pace, only hearing half of what Mrs. Corbin had told him, but only needing to hear that half.

Miss Chorley has not returned from the beach, sir.

It was midway through the afternoon at this point, and she had left shortly after breakfast, as he understood it. The tide would be much higher now than it had been then, and if she was still in the cave, it would be flooding at this point. Not entirely flooded, of course, and especially not as the last few days had been dry, but high enough to make wading out of any of the caves difficult, even for those who could walk with ease.

What had he been thinking, sending her there by herself? If she had come to any injury, he would never forgive himself.

He raced to the nearest path to the beach, not caring about its terrain or incline. He barreled down it, feeling his speed increasing with every single step. He probably could have leapt into the sea itself with this sort of additional propulsion, but he wasn't about to test it. There was only one thought in his mind and one task in his heart.

Getting to Abigail.

Once his feet were on the rocks of the beach, he veered hard to his right, his arms flailing in an almost embarrassing fashion as he sprinted towards the caves.

"ABIGAIL!" he bellowed, unable to stop himself. "Abigail!"

There was no reply, and that was terrifying. Was she unconscious? Were the rising waves drowning her out? Was she trapped so deeply in the caves that she couldn't hear him, or he couldn't hear her? Scenario after scenario raced through his mind, each worse than the last.

His chest seized with a burning pressure he'd never felt before, something that robbed him of breath and made him frantic. For just a moment, he did not want to see inside the cave. Did not want to know what awaited him. Did not want to see what had become of Abigail.

Once he knew, everything would change.

He swallowed hard as he reached the first cave.

He *wanted* everything to change.

Exhaling a short breath, Gilles stepped into the cave, pausing to let his eyes adjust as the sea water slapped around his ankles. "Abigail? Can you hear me?"

"Here."

His heart surged to his throat with a sharp sting of emotion and Gilles continued forward, his eyes darting around frantically. Her voice was choked, weak, and tear-filled, and he loved and hated it in equal measure. He loved hearing her voice however it came, and he hated the pain he heard in it.

Then he saw her, halfway between the cave entrance and the warm pool, collapsed against the wall.

"Abigail," he whispered on a ragged exhale. He moved for her at once, his steps slow and sloshing in the water.

Her eyes never left him as he approached, their blue shade dimmed by the shadows. There was a dark weariness to her features, and her fair hair partially streamed from her typically neat plaits. Her dress was torn and filthy, completely soaked and clinging to her skin, but it was the streaks of red along her skirts that gave him most pause.

She made no move towards him when he reached her, and hardly seemed aware of the water pooling around her legs as she sat there.

He crouched before her, putting one hand on her pale, freezing cheek. "Abigail, *ma douce,* what happened?"

Her mouth tightened into a thin line and her eyes fluttered shut as a tear leaked from one. He was quick to swipe it away with his thumb, but she did not seem to feel it. "I f-fell. So many times. I cannot w-walk anymore, and I could not... I t-tried to pull myself out, but my arms..." She inhaled sharply, broken sobs rippling the sound. "I am not s-strong enough. And I hurt… I *h-hurt,* Gilles, and…" She looked away, more tears streaming now, her entire body shaking.

"Oh, *ma douce,*" Gilles murmured, brushing his thumb across her cheek again. "Come on. Let's get you home."

Without waiting for her reaction or participation, he reached both arms beneath her and hauled her up, cradling her trembling form.

Abigail turned her face towards his chest, continuing to sob as both of her hands gripped his shirt. He could feel the iciness of her entire body as she curled more fully into him, and it was all he could do not to gasp at the waves of cold it sent through his own. He said nothing as he carried her out of the cave, but her wordless whimpers, choked with the tears that splashed onto his shoulder, were impossible to ignore.

He pulled her closer, his mouth at her ear. "Shh, *ma chérie. Tout va bien. Tu es en sécurité maintenant. Je te tiens. Tiens-toi à moi. Je te tiens. Je te tiens. Je ne te laisserai pas partir.*"

She continued to shiver against him, but her cries softened the more he murmured. He couldn't even be sure what he was telling her, as the words simply tumbled from his lips. He was saying anything and everything to soothe her, and if it worked, he would keep saying it.

The path back up to his lands was more difficult with Abigail in his arms, but she was light enough that it was only awkward, not strenuous. And he didn't dare take the longer path, even if it would be easier on him. No, he needed to get her back to the house as soon as possible, and he would have climbed up a mountain with her in his arms if he had to.

Abigail began to shake again, this time more viciously than a simple series of shivers from cold. This was a full body trembling, and that frightened him more than anything yet. He hefted her a little closer, letting her brow touch his neck and immediately hissing at the warmth he felt there.

Where all the rest of her skin was cold and clammy, her brow could have seared him by comparison.

He crested the top of the path and started running towards

Coutanche as fast as he could without jostling Abigail too badly. "Mrs. Corbin! Mrs. Corbin!" he bellowed as he ran.

Abigail moaned softly, her grip on his shirt loosening almost entirely, her still-trembling body going almost completely lifeless in his arms.

He pressed his lips to her brow as his heart thundered in his ears. "Hold on, *ma douce*. Hold on."

There was no response.

Mrs. Corbin met him at the door, her eyes going round as she took in Abigail in his arms. "Miss Chorley? What happened, sir?"

"I don't know yet," Gilles huffed as she stepped back to let him through. "She said something about falling and she couldn't stand, and the cave was flooding…" He met the housekeeper's eyes. "She's burning up and her body is freezing, and she won't stop shaking."

That seemed to break through Mrs. Corbin's shock. "Right, then. To her rooms." She turned on her heel and started striding down the corridor ahead of him. "Sally! Send for Dr. Bisset!"

Gilles followed hard on her heels, feeling as though Abigail might turn into ice in his arms.

Mrs. Corbin barked further orders at the few maids they had, instructing one to have the fire stoked up in Abigail's room, to have toweling and linens warmed, to have extra blankets brought into her room. Order after order that whipped by his ears without actually sinking into his mind. He thought he heard something about keeping his daughters in the nursery, but that might have only been an idea in his mind that sounded like Mrs. Corbin's authoritative voice.

They entered Abigail's rooms, and one of the maids on the receiving end of Mrs. Corbin's bellowing was hard at work stoking up the fire. Gilles deposited Abigail on the bed, brushing her hair back from her face. She still trembled, but her eyes remained closed, and she made no sound but for the insensible whimpers from somewhere deep within her.

"Sir."

Cieux, but she was beautiful. He hated to see her like this, so fragile and lifeless, but everything about her was exquisite. He could barely breathe for the thundering of his heart right now, his panic vanishing into a bath of fire as he looked at her now.

"Sir."

Why hadn't he taken the time to really look at her before? He'd seen the woman sitting with his daughters in the library only days ago, the one with an impish light in her brilliant eyes. The one who could make his girls giggle with such ease and light. The one who could laugh with him over trivial points in *The Odyssey*. The one who seemed to actually see him.

She saw him.

No one had really seen him since Heloise, and he wanted…

He wanted…

"MR. BICHARD."

Gilles blinked and looked at Mrs. Corbin across the bed. "What?"

She jerked her head towards the door.

"No," he ground out. "I am not leaving her."

Mrs. Corbin exhaled very shortly. "Sir, we need to strip her out of these wet things and get her into some fresh and warm things. Unless you would like to embarrass the girl while she's insensible like this, which I will not permit, either turn your back or leave the room."

He stood there uncertainly, still adamant that he could not leave her, but certainly not wanting to do anything he would have to explain later. Anything to mortify her or make her feel more vulnerable than she already had been in the caves. But how could he…? *How* could he…?

He looked at Abigail's unconscious, shaking, freezing form, swallowing hard and wondering where these tears on his cheeks had come from. He looked back at Mrs. Corbin, feeling as helpless as a child.

Her expression softened as she looked at him, and she tsked softly. "You can come back in as soon as she's decent. Go change out of your own wet things. Knock first and wait for me to answer." Her look was severe, but he saw her own eyes misting and her throat bobbing.

That gave him more direction than anything else.

With a final brush of his fingers against Abigail's icy cheek, Gilles turned from the bed and stalked out of the room, his hands quickly forming fists at his sides. His mind—determined to torment him—

replayed every aching moment from the cave. The sound of Abigail's response to him, like heavenly music after the fearful silence and yet raking his soul across imaginary coals. The haunted, glazed look in her eyes that meant she didn't seem to actually see him. Or anything at all. The blood…

Gilles cursed as he entered his rooms and began to strip off his own clothing. What kind of injury would a woman like Abigail have to endure in order to be entirely incapable of walking? He knew how strong she was, limp or no limp. He had seen how she managed from day to day, and there was nothing fragile or delicate about her. Anyone with half of a brain and a single functioning eye could tell she had remarkable inner strength and perseverance, as well as a willpower to rival any in the world. Her ability to endure pain was evident the moment one learned of what she had already been through, and yet she had never complained of daily pain, though she must have had it. The only indication he'd ever had of pain from her was the day the girls climbed on her legs.

That was it. There was never any other discussion of pain, discomfort, or required adjustments. Aside from his witnessing her trouble with the path to the beach that day, there was never anything else.

To see *that* woman brought so low. So vulnerable. So desperate. So lifeless.

It was harrowing, horrifying, and humbling.

And now he was beginning to shake in a way that had nothing to do with damp clothing.

Half dressed in dry clothing, Gilles sank onto his bed, his face going into his hands as shudders raced up and down his spine at the speed of lightning. He wasn't sure what he felt for Abigail, but it was a hell of a lot more than he'd ever expected to feel for any woman ever again. Worst of all, there wasn't any vengeance to claim in this. There was no person to blame, no creature to shake his fist at, and not a single way to make any of it better.

Just as it had been with Heloise.

There was only the overwhelming feeling of helplessness.

He didn't love Abigail, that much he knew. Not yet.

But he wanted to. And he was fairly certain he was going to.

Which was exhilarating and terrifying.

And it made seeing her in this weakened, diminished capacity even more difficult. He couldn't leave her alone for long. He would not.

Pushing himself off his bed once more, he hurried into a clean linen shirt, shoving it into his trousers as he moved out of his room. He didn't even bother with footwear or a weskit, let alone a cravat. He was decently dressed for his own house and to look in on the woman he was going to love while she was injured and unwell. He didn't care about anything else.

He knocked at the door firmly, holding his breath.

"Not yet, sir," Mrs. Corbin called back. "Almost. If you could see if the doctor has arrived, it would be most helpful."

Gilles grumbled under his breath, cursing in French at the impossibility of waiting longer to sit by Abigail's bedside. Surely, he could hold her hand while the others did useful things. But no, he was going to make sure the doctor knew where to go instead of leaving one of the maids to do it. And in order to receive the doctor, he would, in fact, require footwear.

He shook his head as he retreated to his room for those items, then obediently went down to the main floor to await Dr. Bisset. Of course, the man had not yet arrived, so Gilles was left to pace almost absently in the interim. Maddening, being separated from Abigail by an entire floor of the house because his housekeeper had determined another course of action for him. She would have her reasons, and he would likely find them perfectly reasonable when he viewed them in retrospect, but for the present, it was nothing short of irritating.

He should have checked Abigail for a head injury. She had mentioned falling, and her weakness had been apparent from almost the first moment he'd seen her. An injury to the head could prove fatal at times. What if he'd missed that?

No, wait, his clothing had not held any blood from the vicinity of where her head had been. There would probably have been blood from a head injury, would there not? He had so little experience with great injuries to the head, only minor ones, which seemed to bleed a great deal.

But her legs… There had certainly been blood on her legs, and quite a bit of it. Why had he not checked her legs before getting her out?

He shook his head at himself, the scolding hot on the action's heels. He hadn't checked her legs because she had been distressed and the cave flooding. He'd needed to get her out, and he had done so. That had been the priority. He hadn't considered blood loss or fever at the time, only safety.

Now that she was safe, it was her health that concerned him most. He knew only too well how quickly one's health could deteriorate under the right conditions. He could not endure that again, even with someone he… someone whom…

He just could not.

Footsteps sounded from the gravel drive and Gilles whirled on his heel to face the approaching doctor. "Dr. Bisset, thank you for coming so quickly."

The doctor was a relative neighbor of Coutanche House and had been the one to tend Heloise in her last days, and he had always been kind but forthright. Gilles was counting on exactly the same sort of exchanges with Abigail's condition.

"Mr. Bichard." He shook Gilles's hand and walked with him to the stairs. "Who is unwell?"

"My—our governess," Gilles corrected quickly. "She was at the cave with the warm pool this morning to exercise her leg, which was damaged badly some years ago. She was delayed returning home, so I went down to the beach to search for her. I found her very injured, wet, cold, weak…" He shook his head, exhaling shortly at the reappearance of the tension in his chest. "It was shocking."

Dr. Bisset's high brow creased as he thought, his dark eyes hooded with the motion. "Is she of a delicate constitution?"

Gilles shrugged. "I would not have said so before today, but she felt feverish when I carried her home."

"She was unable to walk on her own?" Dr. Bisset's bushy, greying brows shot up, creating more creases.

Nodding, Gilles gestured down the corridor as they reached the top stair. "She said she tried to pull herself out of the cave. I don't know. I did not get all of the details, I only thought of getting her out of there."

"With good reason." Dr. Bisset sighed and gave Gilles's arm a squeeze. "I will see to it. I take it your girls are fond of her?"

Gilles swallowed with some difficulty. "Very," he managed to reply, leaving out the detail that *he* was fond of her as well.

Very.

Dr. Bisset nodded and knocked on the door, entering when Mrs. Corbin's voice answered affirmatively. Gilles followed silently, a torrent of emotions rocking his core and keeping any one thought or feeling from overriding all the rest.

Abigail was still atop the bedcovers, but she had been changed into a dry, warm nightgown, and she no longer seemed to be shaking. Her hair had been unpinned and brushed out, streaming along the pillows and her shoulders like some sort of halo. Her knees and shins were exposed, reveling angry cuts and abrasions, a few of which still bled from the deep gashes.

And beneath those cuts, abrasions, and blood, Gilles could finally see the scars on her right leg and foot that she had warned him about.

It was worse than he had imagined, and yet not as horrifying as he had feared. The skin of her right leg was uneven and taut in some places, the scars a deeper pink than her natural shade. There was some puckering in certain areas, and various shades of discoloration in her foot as scars crossed most of its surface. It was certainly unsightly, but he would never have called it ugly. Disfiguring, yes, but not disastrous.

It was entirely a testament to what Abigail had survived and endured. Each mark was a witness of her pain and her strength. There was nothing to be ashamed of with them, but he could also understand the desire to keep them covered. The wish to be viewed by others as she had been before. To leave people wondering about the cause of her limp without any indication of her past.

To keep her scars for her eyes alone.

How many times had he been grateful his scars were only on his heart and soul and therefore unseen by anyone else?

Why shouldn't Abigail have the same privacy?

"These wounds are superficial enough to just be bandaged," Dr. Bisset was saying as Gilles tuned back in to the conversation. "The ones just above her knees I will stitch, but they ought to be cleaned first. I am sure some of the rocky debris will have gotten in there."

Mrs. Corbin immediately turned to the maids in the room. "Girls. Bring me a basin of vinegar, water, and some rags. Willow bark tea as well. Go, now."

Gilles smiled to himself as the maids rushed out of the room with a briskness that any general would have appreciated. There was no one like Mrs. Corbin anywhere.

He caught a similar smile on Dr. Bisset's face as the doctor moved towards Abigail's head, his hands going to her face. He checked her eyes, the pulse in her neck, the temperature of her brow. He examined her head, every inch of it, and pressed his fingers gently against the line of her throat on both sides. He listened to her breathing and her heart, felt the pulse in her wrist, checked her mouth.

All without saying much of anything aloud. He muttered all sorts of things to himself, but nothing to Gilles or Mrs. Corbin. He returned his attention to Abigail's legs, pressing up and down and watching her face, for whatever reason. He felt along her ankles, twisting them this way and that, before looking at her hands, examining her abraded palms carefully.

Gilles was starting to grow irritated with the complete lack of information, but he knew better than to interject while the man was conducting an examination. Mostly because he understood that he would be told the man needed to finish his examination before he had answers. Yet somehow, knowing that did nothing to settle him, and he began to wonder if Dr. Bisset was intentionally extending his examination to either irk him or find more information than was strictly necessary.

Whichever it was, Gilles was reaching the end of his patience, and he hadn't known there was one of those.

The maids returned with the demanded supplies for Mrs. Corbin, who began working in conjunction with Dr. Bisset to cleanse the deeper wounds on Abigail's legs. Flushing the area again and again, ridding the tissue of any impurities that could worsen the fever or Abigail's condition. Then, as though to torment Gilles personally, the doctor began the painstaking process of suturing the wounds. Abigail did not so much as wince throughout the procedure, which frightened Gilles as much as anything else.

Dr. Bisset exhaled loudly as he straightened and turned to them both, smiling gently. "She is feverish and undoubtedly will have quite the dreadful cold when she wakes. As far as I can tell, it is the cold and her exhaustion that rendered her thus. It does not appear that any bones are broken, and her breathing and heart are quite regular. I would suggest getting her fully warmed and tending her wounds and fever for now. Whatever her injury was—whatever her injury is— wounds aside, it is likely soft-tissue related, and I may not have an answer until she is awake and alert enough to tell us what happened and what exactly hurts. Understand me?"

Gilles nodded against a painful swallow even as relief filled him.

"But… but she hasn't woken, Doctor," Mrs. Corbin protested in a soft, motherly way.

Dr. Bisset gave her another smile, this one full of understanding. "Exhaustion, Mrs. Corbin, combined with the cold. She will likely sleep the rest of today and through the night. I wouldn't leave her alone in case she should take a turn with her fever, but as of this moment, I do not see any great reason for concern."

There was something inherently calming about Dr. Bisset's manner, Gilles would not deny it, and he found himself relaxing the more he listened, knowing full well the man would have acted swiftly had there been any danger.

It didn't change the present feeling of helplessness plaguing him, but at least the panic was ebbing away.

Dr. Bisset nodded and turned to him. "Send for me when she's awake. Truly awake, you understand, not small intervals between sleeping."

Gilles gave him a quick nod and started to go to the door, but the doctor stopped him, gripping his arm firmly. Gilles looked at his hand, then up into the man's face.

He nudged his head back towards the bed, his mouth curving in a knowing smile. "I can see myself out, Bichard. It's fine." He released his arm, patting it in a friendly manner, then left the room.

Gilles stared after him, wondering what Dr. Bisset had seen in his expression or manner that made him think… that gave him any indication that…

He heard Abigail moan weakly, the sound shaky as it was emitted, and turned quickly towards the bed.

Her body was shaking from head to toe, her jaw and teeth chattering frantically.

"Blankets, girls!" Mrs. Corbin bellowed, the sound making Abigail flinch. "Where are those blasted blankets?"

Gilles did not think, did not wait, and moved onto the bed, lying beside Abigail and pulling her into his arms as he pressed his legs against hers, rubbing his hands up and down her back rapidly. *"Ses blessures. Soignez ses blessures,"* he insisted, gesturing to her legs. "Clean them. Bandage them. Then warm her feet."

Mrs. Corbin was nodding as she began to rub the bottom of Abigail's feet. "Those slow, lazy girls. I should have them both lashed for their tardiness."

Gilles smiled at her as he continued to try and warm Abigail. He knew full well that his housekeeper would never raise a hand or a lash to anyone at Coutanche, no matter what she threatened. It was her brusque, bristling manner to hide the caring nature of her heart, and everybody knew it.

Together, they would set Abigail to rights. She would be well soon enough, and then Gilles could move forward in whatever direction felt right.

Such as loving her.

Chapter Eleven

$\mathcal{A}$bby had never been a very good patient, and she was not likely to start now. Two days she had been abed, and she was finally able to not feel as though death had frozen her and then thawed her out.

The trouble was that Mrs. Corbin refused to let her leave the bed, and thus Abby was bored, restless, and terribly stiff.

Not a lovely combination.

"I am *fine*, Mrs. Corbin," she ground out as the woman fussed over her bedcovers for the forty-seventh time. "No fever. Check."

Tutting softly, Mrs. Corbin reached over and touched her brow with the back of her hand, then did the same with her cheek. "True, but you've only just managed a full bowl of broth for a meal. You haven't the strength to do anything more. So you shall stay in bed."

Abby flopped back against the pillows in irritation, which didn't do much, as the pillows had been so piled up for her that she was still mostly sitting up. "I want to move!"

"Move in your bed, Abigail," the housekeeper said without concern, gesturing to the mattress. "Plenty of space."

Normally, Abby was a perfectly behaved adult and an elegant woman, but the present circumstances washed all of that away, and she glowered at Mrs. Corbin like a petulant schoolgirl without any shame whatsoever.

If that bothered Mrs. Corbin, she made no indication. She chuckled softly and put a hand on her hip, raising a brow at Abby. "You can pout all you want, child, but I am not the one who was shaking like a leaf for an entire day no matter what we did to warm you. You scared us all to hell and back again, and I will not apologize for being strict with your recovery. Why, Mr. Bichard held you for ten hours straight and slept just there, sweating his blessed hair off just to make sure you were warm enough."

Abby felt her eyes widen, painfully so, as her mouth fell open. "He did what?"

Mrs. Corbin blinked and bustled towards the door. "Yes, well, we all did our best to take care of you, and I am delighted you are feeling well, but I insist on your remaining abed today. No excuses."

Abby didn't even have it within her to argue the point as she watched the woman leave her room.

She barely recollected what happened the day at the caves after she realized she could not drag herself back to Coutanche. She had been so tired, so cold, and the water had begun to flood in. She vaguely remembered Gilles coming and the warm burst at seeing him there in front of her, but the warmth evaporated quickly in the face of the ice that had begun to fill her body. She knew he had picked her up and carried her out, and it was only then that she had given in to the darkness that had been encroaching on her.

After that, she just remembered everything being dark and cold for ages. She was asleep, but not dreaming, and she could feel the cold in every part of her body. There were moments of warmth, and she knew someone had said soothing words to her that chased some of the darkness away, but none of it was clear. None of it made sense. Eventually, the coldness faded, and she had the warmth they were all apparently trying to give her, and then her sleep went deeper, and she hadn't been aware of anything until she woke some time later.

Dr. Bisset had visited her yesterday and looked over everything, declaring it satisfactory, but asked her to be gentle with herself. He had checked her legs and determined she had certainly sprained both knees, though she might not know how severely until she tried to walk again. He was a kind man and told his opinion rather frankly, which she appreciated. She had never liked the doctors who simpered and spoke abstractly about whatever they were doing and thinking, as though a female mind could not possibly comprehend medical details.

At any rate, Abby had been assured she was not overly ill and should recover quickly.

She was personally convinced that she would recover far more quickly if she were not treated like an invalid, but that was apparently neither here nor there.

A faint shuffling brought Abby's attention up, and she smiled at the sight of two little faces trying to peek through the slit in the barely ajar door.

"Come in, *mes filles,*" she invited, waving them over. "I need some cuddles."

Giggling, Madeline and Marie-Claire pushed the door open and bounded onto her bed, clambering to either side of her, carefully avoiding her legs. They nestled against her eagerly, and Marie-Claire surprised her by wrapping both arms around her waist and holding tight.

Abby smiled down at her and began stroking her curls. "Everything all right, little one?"

Marie-Claire shook her head fiercely.

"No? Why not, sweetling?" she asked, kissing her head softly.

"Scared," Marie-Claire mumbled as she clung to Abby, hiding her face against her side.

Abby blinked, her smile wavering. "Scared? Of what?"

"We thought you were dying," Madeline said in a quiet voice, her fingers tracing absent patterns on the coverlet. "Marie-Claire doesn't really remember when Maman died, but I do. I know people die and go away forever. I wasn't that scared, but she was."

Marie-Claire made a soft whimpering sound against Abby's nightgown.

"Oh, *mes filles…*" She sighed and pulled them both closer, leaning back on her pillows a little as her eyes began to burn with tears. "I promise you, I was not going to die. I was unwell, but not that unwell. Just very tired and hurt, and very, very cold. Did you think the doctor came because I was dying?"

Madeline shrugged, not looking at her, but she felt Marie-Claire nod.

She kissed both of their heads quickly. "Sometimes," she said after an emotional pause, "a doctor just comes because he can help someone to feel better. Or to help us know what is wrong. Did your papa or Mrs. Corbin tell you that I hurt my legs, too?"

"Oui," Marie-Claire said softly, shifting her face to at least make her words more clear.

"Dr. Bisset looked at the places where I hurt my legs to see if I needed some help to get better," Abby explained, keeping her tone as light as possible. "Two of them needed a little help, but they are going to be just fine. And I don't even have a fever anymore. Feel my head, see if it's warm at all."

Both girls sat up and felt her forehead, though Abby doubted they would have known if she had a fever at all, unless it was raging out of control. Still, anything she could do to alleviate their fears would be good. The idea that they feared so much was devastating.

"See?" Abby pressed when they both dropped their hands. "I am well now."

Madeline frowned, her expression so like her father's that it was endearing. "Then why are you still in bed?"

Abby smiled and brushed the girl's hair back a little. "Because Mrs. Corbin won't let me get up!" she whispered loudly, making a scared face.

Both girls giggled at that, and Marie-Claire sat back, looking up at her. "Nobody argues with Mrs. Corbin," she vowed seriously, still smiling.

"I know," Abby assured her. "That's why I'm afraid to get out of bed on my own."

Again the girls laughed, and only the sound of the door pushing open farther broke their giggles.

Gilles stood in the doorway, smiling at the scene, his blue eyes crinkling in their usual handsome way. He wore no coat, only his shirt and weskit, without even a cravat for decoration. And there was something softer in his smile that Abby did not quite understand.

Something that made her heart skip several beats and her cheeks flush, as well as created a strange dryness in her throat.

Which, of course, made her want to swallow, which was rather difficult.

"I see the patient is well enough for visitors," Gilles murmured, his smile turning crooked. "Might I enter?"

Abby nodded jerkily. "Please do, sir." She looked at the girls, who were beaming at their father, and felt herself settle marginally.

"Though I fear there is no more space on the bed. You will have to make do with a chair."

That made the girls laugh again, their merriment the most delightful music in the world.

Gilles paused in the act of coming over, his eyes latched on to Abby's, and his smile deepened. "Ah, well, I suppose I may endure suffering such an indignity. This time." He gave his daughters a look of mock severity that only made their giggles worse.

Abby beamed at his playing along, her heart still skipping its own little jig in her chest as he situated himself in a chair near her bed. He winked at her, still smiling and looking perfectly at ease.

"Papa, she has no fever," Marie-Claire reported with a smile, leaning back against Abby.

"*Très bien, ma fée,*" he replied. "And are her hands cold?"

The girls quickly gripped her hands to check. "No," Madeline said quickly.

He cupped his chin, making a show of pretending to think. "What about her cheeks? Are they hot or cold? Or just right?"

Small hands clapped onto Abby's face again, making her laugh loudly.

"Just right!" her little would-be doctors announced.

"Is her nose cold, Mariette?"

Marie-Claire put her palm to Abby's nose, snickering as she did so. "A little cold."

"Hmm."

Abby glanced over at Gilles, seeing him putting his own palm to his nose.

He frowned. "Mine is, too, so I don't think that counts."

Madeline fell back on the mattress, giggling incessantly as her arms wrapped around her stomach.

Gilles snapped his fingers as though an idea had struck him. "Check her toes! See if her toes are cold!"

The girls immediately scrambled for the bedcovers before Abby had a chance to protest and she looked at Gilles in distress.

He winked at her again. "You're still bandaged, Abigail. They will see nothing."

Relief had never tasted so sweet, and this was the first time Abby could actually recall *tasting* relief on her tongue.

And it was almost as sweet as Gilles knowing exactly what she had been afraid of and already knowing it would be fine.

Her cheeks flamed with heat as she waited for the girls to cover her toes with their hands and give their answer to their father.

"They're warm!" Marie-Claire told them all.

"Whew!" Gilles wiped at his non-perspiring brow. "You had better cover her legs and feet now, *mes chéris,* to make sure they stay that way."

The girls quickly pulled the bedcovers back over Abby's legs, tucking her in like she was the child and they the doting mothers or nannies.

It was adorable.

When Abby was perfectly encased in the fabric, practically unable to move, the girls looked at their father for further instructions.

Gilles was clearly fighting laughter at their expressions, but somehow managed to avoid any sounds of it whatsoever. "Then we must conclude that she is warm enough and healthy enough for you to show her the drawings you made for her to get better."

Both girls gasped, looking at each other in delight, and bolted from the bed as well as the room, barreling out of control towards their nursery.

Abby snorted softly, biting down on her lip hard to keep from laughing any louder, casting her eyes to Gilles as she did so.

He sat back in his chair, his mouth curved in a wide, crooked grin, his eyes delightfully crinkled. "They should be a few minutes," he whispered loudly. "They don't remember where they put them."

Fighting laughter again, Abby put a hand over her eyes, shaking now with mirth. Then the shaking became something else entirely, her eyes burning again with tears that fell as rapidly as they formed.

"Abigail?" She heard Gilles move from his chair and felt the mattress beside her dip, then the brush of his arm against hers as he sat beside her. *"Ma douce,* what's wrong?"

She shook her head, hissing her breath in and out between nearly clenched teeth. "Th-they thought I was going to d-die, Gilles. Marie-Claire was afraid. And Madeline… She said she knows people die and go away, and she's trying so hard to be strong and accept it, but they… Oh, they are breaking my heart, and I can't…"

"Shh, shh, come now, *ma douce*…" He wrapped his arms around her and pulled her into his chest tightly. His lips pressed against her hair, then rested there. "I thought we might lose you, too, you know. When I first brought you back. I have seen death far more often than they have, and I was almost sure it was coming again. It was not until you were awake and aware of the conversations around you that I truly believed you were safe."

Abby sniffled, her tremors easing but not subsiding entirely as she listened to his low, soothing voice and felt his words against her hair. It was like slipping into the warm pool again, but gentler and more consuming of everything she was. This was… right. Natural. Easy.

Home.

She shuddered in his hold, allowing herself to lean further into him as the truth sank into her. Being in his arms felt like home.

She did not have a home anymore apart from the school, and that was certainly where she was most comfortable, but it was also her identity and her life's work. Here she was, for all intents and purposes, a governess and nothing more or less than Abigail Chorley ever was. Gilles only knew the woman she pretended to be, and she was only pretending her name and her aims for being here. Everything else was entirely her.

And he only knew her as that person.

And somehow it was enough.

Ma douce.

My sweet.

It was an unexpected endearment, and perhaps inappropriate for an employer to use with her, but it did not feel like she was being cared for and embraced by her employer.

Not in the slightest.

"I am so relieved you are safe," Gilles whispered, his chest rumbling with the words. "And well. And whole. You have no idea how I… what I… but even I cannot comprehend how terrified you must have been, *ma douce*."

His hands began to run over her hair and her back, his fingers tangling in her long, unbound tresses. The motions were almost hypnotic, sending fiery ripples of pleasure down her back and into the tips of her fingers and toes.

"Will you tell me, Abigail?" he asked, his lips moving temptingly against her hair to her brow. "Tell me what happened."

Abby curled into him, laying her head against his shoulder, her fingers finding the buttons of his weskit and fiddling with them absently. "It was really rather simple," she murmured, smiling as she replayed the way he said her name over and over in her mind. "I wasn't marking my steps and slipped. I landed on both knees rather hard, and scraped my hands." She held one palm out, looking at the angry scratches and abrasions.

Gilles cupped that palm and brought it to his lips gently.

Her breath stuttered in her lungs, feeling caught on each rib.

He pressed her hand against his heart and nodded against her, saying nothing.

Abby tried to swallow, but it was impossible. "I went into the warm pool afterwards," she said, her voice rasping against her dry throat. "It was magical. There was some pain, but I quickly learned where it was and how to avoid it. I was able to move my leg in ways I never thought I would again. I felt so strong, so capable…" Her voice caught as she recalled the thrill and excitement she had felt, the dreams that had opened back up, the hope that had filled her soul…

Gilles continued running his fingers through her hair, murmuring wordlessly against her brow when she didn't go on.

Shaking her head, Abby exhaled slowly. "It was amazing. I got out and determined I would come back often and try to get better and better, perhaps ridding myself of my limp one day. Then I would no longer be a cripple."

"Don't call yourself that, *ma douce,*" Gilles whispered, his arms tightening around her. "Please."

His words sank heat into her heart, making her shiver in his hold. "But… while I was redressing, I fell again. Slipped, but also… my bad leg gave out. It must have been fatigued from the work I did, and from the fall before. I hit the ground, harder than the first time, and fell into the pool again. I could barely get out that time. My legs wouldn't sustain the effort, so I had to pull myself out. And I could not stand after that. Not even on my good leg, so I tried to crawl. And then I couldn't even do that. I couldn't get out. I was just w-waiting, and then the w-water started coming in…"

Gilles tucked her head under his chin then, his arms enveloping her so completely, she felt as though she might actually melt into his body. His heat warmed the echoes of her chilled memories, reminded her she was safe and whole here. The beating of his heart tapped a steady, lulling cadence against her hands, pulsing life into her skin. His hold was so secure, so comforting, so invigorating…

Home, she had called it.

Yes. Yes, this was home.

He was home.

"I am so sorry, Abigail," Gilles said softly. "Sorry for your experience. Sorry I did not think to go with you. Sorry it took me so long to realize…"

"Don't apologize," Abigail insisted before he could say more. "How could you have known? I am stubborn and determined to not be fragile or a victim. I ought to have realized that it would be wise for someone else to be with me. If I did not have more pride than sense, I might have seen… I might have avoided… But accepting limitations has never been something I can do easily. I should, considering I am… Well, that I am now…"

He pulled back and looked at her closely, his eyes searching hers. One of his hands moved to her cheek, the other still on the back of her head. "You have more strength than anyone I have ever known, Abigail. You are not fragile, nor weak, if that was going to come out of your mouth in the near future. Anyone could have suffered injury down there, and many have, even with remarkable physical strength or stature. There is nothing wrong with you. Nothing. Do you believe me?"

"No," Abby whispered, a pair of tears falling from her eyes. "I know myself too well."

He brushed her tears away, exhaling slowly. "But you do not see. You cannot." He smiled softly, his thumb stroking her cheek.

"Mr. Bichard…" she whispered, her heart thundering in her ears and throat at the tenderness she saw in his eyes.

His smile turned rather wry. "I think we are beyond mister or miss anything by now, don't you, Abigail?" He leaned closer, pausing just a moment before his lips gently touched hers.

She stilled at the contact, unaware of breath or pulse or light or anything but the feeling of his mouth. She could not move, could not think.

He waited a moment, and when she did not pull away, he kissed her again, leaning more fully into it, his mouth grazing hers and tenderly pulling at her lips again and again. Slowly, almost painfully slowly, but so very exquisitely.

She shivered again, this time from head to toe and without any sort of chill whatsoever.

His lips parted from hers, hovering just a breath away.

"Gilles…" she breathed, shaking in his hold.

He laughed very softly. "I could not help myself," he murmured as his nose brushed hers. "Should I apologize, Abigail?"

Abby reached up, her fingers curling around his wrist and keeping his hold on her face. "No."

She felt his smile as his lips took hers yet again, no less tenderly, but with more certainty and more feeling, and now, filled with the fire that only he had ever stoked, she kissed him in return.

Chapter Twelve

*H*ow Gilles managed to do anything at all after kissing Abigail was completely beyond him. And she had returned the attentions so sweetly, so perfectly, that he was entirely unmanned by it. He'd have kissed her for hours had his girls not returned shortly after they had begun, and he'd been relegated back to his chair for the duration of the interlude.

It had taken all of his strength not to rush back into her room and continue showering her with his kisses for the rest of the day.

But he had managed.

Today, however…

Well, he had not rushed in there. Had not even seen her yet.

But he was considering it.

Seriously.

But there was work to be done, unfortunately, and if he wanted to maintain any sort of connection with England or France, he had to do it.

Then he could proceed with kissing Abigail.

If she wished it.

What if she did not wish it?

Gilles groaned and shoved his hands into his hair, dropping his elbows onto the surface of his desk. Why must falling in love with someone be so damned complicated? He was overthinking everything and questioning possibilities and losing his once-thriving mind.

It had not helped that his dreams had been all of Abigail, making sleeping torture, but there was nothing to be done about it now.

"Work first," he ground out to himself. "Her later."

It was not even remotely convincing for his heart, his body, or his mind. But tormenting himself was not an option either.

He growled and reached for his desk drawer, pulling it out sharply and retrieving the latest stack of letters there.

They were back to being vague, even within the code, and he did not like that. It had been a few months since things had been so carefully worded, and he'd never heard the results of whatever operation that had been, either. No one was coming out and saying what they meant, what was going on, what anyone ought to do, and yet somehow those involved in writing these letters back and forth had enough understanding to not question it.

Gilles knew there were others doing as he was doing and forwarding letters along for the cause, so he had no doubt that other letters had other details, and he knew all too well that meetings took place between supporters and operatives frequently. Those meetings likely held all of the information he was missing with this particular arrangement, but it was maddening not to have much to share with his British contacts.

He felt utterly useless in the grander scope of things, and useless was not something he enjoyed being.

He looked over the two letters containing the vague references now, having already decoded them. Between the original letters and the decoded message, he could not find anything resembling insight, and he wondered if something might have changed. Were they double-layering letters once more? That had been agony on his part, but Heloise had managed to crack the additional layer easily. Her mind had always been rapid and keen, so it had never surprised him that she had seen the puzzle for what it was.

Gilles, on the other hand…

He sighed and rubbed at his brow. What did they mean by "candidates," and how could they be "sifting the grain" with them? He knew full well that "clasping hands with friends" meant they were working with supporters of influence for whatever it was, but it hardly gave him direction. There was mention of a foiled attempt, but an attempt at what? The only thing he could safely say was that the pressure exerted by the quill in writing the words "foiled attempt" as well as "missing rodent" was far more intense than any other words in the letter.

"Missing rodent" made no sense, but it must relate to the foiled attempt, whatever it had been. For the corresponding men, their manner of penmanship was always light and neat, so for the excess ink and almost tearing of the parchment in these ones to be noticed now indicated strong emotion indeed. Anger, if he understood it right. Fury, even.

The lack of detail surrounding a fury for the Faction was gnawing at him.

What could be so secretive that it did not warrant clarity in letter? They never spoke vaguely of shipments of arms, smuggling of brandy, transportation of operatives, or locations to meet, and he had passed all of that information on when it came to him. But this? What was so crucial about this that even between trusted contacts, the exact wording could not be used?

He did see one word that he did not care for, however.

"Eliminate."

The word was only used with respect to the missing rodent, but it still made his skin crawl. Whoever the missing rodent was, they were hunting him and would kill him, and quite possibly remove his very existence from history. He had seen such things done in the past, and knew only too well how capable the darker parts of the Faction's contacts could be.

It would certainly be worth warning someone in England about if he had any sort of specifics or insight, but as he did not, he would simply have to sit here in the knowledge that someone was soon going to be done away with for whatever had failed.

But that was unacceptable.

There *had* to be something he could use. Something more.

What was the layering code they had used? What else could there be lurking here?

Punctuation marks.

Gilles felt his smile curl almost viciously as he recalled that, and went to work on a separate sheet of parchment, writing down every letter after a punctuation mark, however strange it seemed. When that was done, he went to the salutation of the letter, which had always been the code for this cipher. Layering ciphers within already layered ciphers. Would life never settle?

He worked at the decryption of the two letters for a while, and only when both were complete did he sit back to read what was there.

Allred cannot be found. Suspect Austria or Spain. Key insists on setting up next bride quickly. Use any means necessary to blackmail.

What in the world any of them would want a bride for was beyond Gilles's comprehension. Especially when the two men writing this correspondence certainly had wives already. And who in the world was Allred? The rodent, naturally, but *who?*

He turned to the next letter.

Two potentials found. Social connections excellent, financial situation bordering desperate. Leaning on government connections for further information. Secondary warehouse secured south of Thames.

Now that was interesting. They already had several warehouses on the south shore of the Thames that they used frequently, not to mention their more particular north shore warehouses. The southern ones were more secret and more protected, but there were plenty to choose from. When they said secured, did they mean a new one had been acquired? Or a specific one they already owned was readied for something?

Still, it was usable information, which was more than he had before.

He pulled out another few sheets of parchment and jotted down a note to Iris, inviting her to inspect the warehouses in her sector. She'd get the information to Briar, as the two of them had different interests in the warehouses and shipping in that area. Then he scribbled out a short note to Trick, this time about the name Allred and the details he'd uncovered there. If Trick was not the one who needed that information, he would see that it got to those who would.

He could do no less than that.

And now that he'd seen this other layer of coding, he needed to go back to his other vague letters and see what else lay there.

Marvelous.

He put his two notes for England into a pouch that he would take down to his contact later that night, and then put his Faction letters into the pouch he would take to that contact in the morning.

He needed his notes to Iris and Trick to arrive before the Faction letters, just in case anything was urgent. If he uncovered more information in the older letters that needed to be sent along with them, he could do that as well, but he doubted anything would be as significant. More than likely just the same information and vagueness.

It would have been so much easier if he could actually sit down with Trick or Iris and show them what he had. They would have far more insight than he did. But it wasn't possible for him to leave Guernsey when Abigail was just barely recovered. She was in no condition to have full care of the girls for however long his trip would take. He had gone away to France for a few days before, and that had always worked well, but he hadn't done that much at all since Heloise had died. He hated leaving the girls alone without a parent in residence.

Besides, he'd never met Trick or Iris in the flesh, and it was safer that way. More frustrating, but safer. No one had ever asked him to go to England, and he had never offered.

But one of these days, he would have to do something more than write about what he was finding.

For the next few hours, Gilles went through every letter that he'd found annoyingly vague and applied the same old code and cipher to the words. As he suspected, there was nothing new to them for the most part, just the same madness about Allred, brides, and warehouses. There was a link missing here that he did not seem to have the key for, and working with incomplete information was one of the most maddening aspects of his position.

But there was an intriguing hint about preparing a channel, and that one was new.

No other letter had ever mentioned anything about a channel. Ever.

What channel were they talking about? How could it be prepared? He could only presume it was related to Allred, the warehouses, and whatever brides were being selected, since those were the threads of the secret correspondence. But anything to do with the warehouses already had a channel out of London, and that route was perfectly secure.

He'd made sure it was secure, and Trick had helped him do so.

His heart slowed to an ominous pounding that soon enveloped his hearing as his mind flicked a new idea alight.

Not *a* channel. *The* Channel.

Guernsey was a Channel Island.

He was the Channel.

They were going to send something—likely someone—to him. The largest cave beneath his home led to a long-abandoned cellar that they had used a few times to filter operatives in and out, but it had been some time since he'd done that. Three years, if his math was correct. He only had to house them there long enough for the proper transportation to either England or France came, and it was a straightforward enough business. Whatever they told him, he relayed to Trick, and the information was acted upon.

But if he was to be housing someone, why hadn't he been notified yet?

He looked back at his most recent work, scanning quickly. Were they planning on bringing the bride, whoever she was, to him?

Oh, *zut*, was his home going to become the hiding place for an elopement?

Gilles snorted a laugh of disbelief and covered his eyes, slumping back against his chair and letting the parchment pages fall to his desk. That was, without a doubt, the stupidest thing he had ever conjectured about anything the Faction could or would do. The worst of it was that it was not even far-fetched, based on the information in the letters. It was entirely possible that, for whatever reason, someone within the Faction was trying to elope, and the Faction was working hard to help them do so.

This was idiotic, and he wasn't going to pretend otherwise.

Glancing at the clock on the mantle, Gilles sighed. Abigail and his daughters would be taking an afternoon meal now, probably with their own tea service. It had been several hours since his early breakfast, and there were several more hours until dinner. He did not usually make a habit of interrupting the structure of his daughters' day, but today he might have to make an exception. He was hungry— for the sight of Abigail as much as for whatever food might be available to him.

Besides, nothing else would get done today unless he took a

break to let his mind reset.

Elopement, indeed. What a nonsensical thought.

Gilles pushed up from his desk and placed all of the letters in his secure hiding place, then strode out of his study in search of his three favorite ladies.

It didn't take long, as the sound of giggles filled the air as soon as he was on the ground floor. That boded well for everyone. No one could make the girls laugh like Abigail, and if they were laughing down here, then she must be out of bed. He'd hoped that would be the case, as she had looked much better the day before, but one could never be entirely certain that recovery would be consistent from day to day.

But Abigail did not belong in a bed like an invalid; she belonged out in the world and among the living, daring Fate to try its best with her and proving herself more than up to the challenge.

The laughter grew louder and more delighted the closer to the dining room Gilles got, and his smile was impossible to restrain at hearing it. His daughters were the light of his life, and their amusement so pure and infectious. If he were at the brink of hell itself, that sound could restore him to life and heaven in an instant. He would need nothing else. And quite honestly, if their laughter were the only music that ever filled his life, he would consider that life well-lived.

He slowed his step as he reached the dining room, not wanting to disturb whatever entertainment was taking place within.

Abigail was telling a story, it seemed, in between bites of their repast, and was taking great creative liberties with the voices she used for each character. Presently, she was portraying a princess, but her voice was a squeaking, lilting Irish accent. Then, without warning, she became the lady-in-waiting, and her voice was a drunken growl that ought to have belonged to a Cockney man. The discrepancies between characters and her portrayals of them were what was causing the utter hilarity, and he was not unmoved by that.

He let himself rest against the door of the dining room, now perfectly visible but still silent, and no one had noticed his entrance as yet. He watched Abigail tell the story with great animation in her face and her movements, somehow still managing to eat while she did so. The girls, on the other hand, were barely managing single bites, with their abject adoration and merry giggles taking their full attention.

Abigail was a vision of loveliness, even with her expressive antics. Her cheeks were rich with healthy color, her eyes vibrant in the afternoon sunlight, and she'd only pulled her hair halfway up, leaving plenty of gorgeous, waving tresses to drape around her shoulders. His fingers itched to run through them just as they had yesterday, and he folded his arms tightly to avoid the temptation to do just that.

He couldn't interrupt the story, after all.

"And then the princess went out to the garden, and who should she see but..." Abigail trailed off, looking between the girls expectantly.

"A goat!" Marie-Claire cried out.

Gilles barked a laugh at Abigail's startled expression, which brought all three of them around to look at him. He clamped his lips together against further laughter and held up an apologetic hand.

Abigail stared at him with wide eyes, seeming just as startled by his presence as his daughter's suggestion. And her cheeks took on a new shade of pink.

What a delightful bit of artwork that was.

A strange smugness began to build in Gilles's chest. Something altogether foreign and particularly tantalizing, and it made him want to do something between playing and prowling. Just to see what might happen.

So he started to walk towards the table slowly, almost ambling, keeping his eyes on Abigail.

She was fixed on him, her attention never wavering, the expression in her eyes as unreadable as the line of her mouth, and only the color of her cheeks gave anything away.

"Mademoiselle Abby," Marie-Claire said, shaking her arm a little. "A goat. Keep going."

Abigail swallowed, her eyes shifting slowly back to the girls. "A... a goat. Right, yes." She cleared her throat before continuing. "The goat did not belong in the garden, of course, so the princess asked..."

Gilles reached the table and picked up the plate next to Madeline, his gaze never straying from Abigail.

"She… she asked, 'What are you doing in here?'" Abigail went on, her voice not quite matching the previous tone the princess held.

"That's not how she speaks, Mademoiselle Abby," Madeline pointed out.

Gilles raised a brow at her as he began to layer slices of cold ham onto his plate.

"'What are you doing in here?'" Abigail tried again, this time with the right tone, but a bit breathless. And more like she was asking Gilles rather than any princess asking a random goat.

There was no stopping the crooked smile that burst across Gilles's lips at the question, and he caught the struggle to swallow in Abigail's delicate throat.

And was it just his eyes, or was her color growing even rosier?

"And… and the goat said, 'Goats l-love gardens. Everybody knows that.' But the princess didn't know that, of course, or she would never have asked," Abigail managed, giving the goat a very soft, childlike voice that had Marie-Claire snickering.

Gilles nodded his agreement to the story as he moved to the asparagus and placed a few stalks on his plate.

Abigail was still watching him, her eyes never wavering. "But the goat was starting to grow restless," she continued. "Goats do, you know."

That gave him pause, and he tilted his head at her curiously, his smile still in place.

He watched as her cheeks positively flamed.

"Goats don't always kn-know where they stand," she stammered as her eyes flicked back and forth between his.

Gilles put the tongs back on the plate with the asparagus and moved around the far end of the table, watching Abigail carefully.

"So the p-princess watched the goat," she squeaked, swallowing again, her food completely untouched now, "trying to figure out how to help the goat be less restless."

He picked up a roll from the basket and set it on the plate beside everything else.

"Because the princess knew that the g-goat loved the garden so much," she said in a rush, her blush extending down her neck. "And she wanted the goat to be happy."

Gilles nodded at her very slowly, setting his plate down without any sound.

"So the p-princess said—"

"I need to speak to Abigail for a moment," Gilles broke in calmly, startling his daughters.

Madeline groaned loudly. "Papa!"

He smiled, but kept his eyes on Abigail. "Just for a moment, *mes filles*. Abigail, would you come with me please?"

She was out of her seat in a blink, and the two of them walked out of the dining room, breaking their locked gazes for the first time in so long, it might have been a lifetime.

Once out in the corridor, Gilles turned to face Abigail, her eyes bright, her color high, her lips parted as her breath raced audibly between them.

With a groan that might have been both internal as well as external, Gilles took her face in his hands and brought his lips crashing down on hers, backing her against the nearest wall and focusing his entire being on devouring every breath and heartbeat from her. Abigail latched her hands behind his head, her nails digging into his scalp as her mouth did much the same with him, colliding and waltzing and consuming every sentient thought and insensible feeling he'd ever known. There was no beginning and no end to their kisses, just a series of more and more, deeper and sweeter, passionate and tender, something raw and ethereal unleashing and coiling between each connection.

Abigail whimpered as he caught her upper lip gently, and he chuckled at the sound. *"Zut, ma douce,"* he breathed when he released her, his mouth moving to her chin and tracking hungrily down her throat. "I may never get enough."

"Gilles…" she moaned, gripping at his hair and arching her neck for him.

He kissed the juncture of her neck and shoulder tenderly, loving the shiver it caused in her. He ran his nose back up the slender column and brought his mouth to her ear, letting his lips play along the surface a moment. "The way you look at me, Abigail… My whole soul feels alive and seen, and just wants you."

She panted a rough exhale, nodding against his lips. "Yes," she whispered.

He grinned for a moment, wondering what question she thought she was answering, then returned his attention to her mouth. One poignant, wringing kiss, returned so eagerly that his knees began to shake.

"But there is one thing I must ask of you, *ma douce,*" Gilles managed as he forced his mouth away from hers.

She blinked, her eyes a trifle hazy as they met his. "What?"

He brushed his thumbs across her still-blushing cheeks tenderly. "Please don't ever liken me to a princess again. It's not entirely flattering for me."

Her eyes widened a moment before she broke out into the most delightful grin he had ever seen. "How else was I supposed to get you to do something?" she asked with ribbons of giggles in her voice. "I've been dying to see you since last night, and I had no idea how to bring that about."

Gilles stroked her cheeks again, shaking his head in amusement. "Just ask for me, *ma douce*. I fear I am now hopelessly yours." He leaned in again to take her teasing, delicious lips once more.

Chapter Thirteen

Time was running out, and Abby was in far more trouble than she had ever imagined being on this mission.

How could she let this happen? How *did* this happen?

She was in love with her target! Wildly and breathlessly in love with him, and reduced to sneaking moments away from the girls to kiss him until they were both completely disheveled and clawing with a need they dare not sate.

She'd never felt anything like this in her entire life, and it was with the one man she should never have even been tempted by.

It had all come crashing into her of late, and somehow perfectly settled her heart for the prospect of the rest of her life.

Her mind was far more sensible, when it made an appearance amidst the fog of enticement that was Gilles. It knew full well that she had a task to do, and if she did not do it now, she never would. She had sent nothing to Milliner about her time here, not even hints at what she suspected, and now she would have to add a confession that might bring down her entire career.

Was it considered treason if Gilles never found out who she was? What if she found a way to filter his messages to England from the Faction and could continue to help the covert operatives that way? If she could stay here with him and be delirious with love for him, but keep this part of her life and her mind separate and focused on her mission for England, could it work?

It was a stupid question, and even now, she shook her head at herself. She was wandering the ground floor of the house tonight, looking for anything that might tell her if the third cave was actually long enough to lead back here somehow. She was not meant to come here and rusticate, let alone find passion with the master of the house, so she had to give England something.

But she refused to believe that Gilles was as wicked as she'd imagined when she'd arrived. There was no way this man would have accepted marrying Lucy Allred against her will just to join London Society for the Faction. If he was involved at all, he had to be a pawn for the Faction. Possibly against his will and without his knowledge, even.

So was she going to find proof to vindicate Gilles or to save him?

Even that was unclear at the moment, but she could not—would not—sleep until she found something. Anything.

Something that could break her heart or save it. Give her life or end it.

Three days of bliss was all she'd allowed herself. Two nights of tossing and turning in her sleep because of the torment and confusion. The conflict between body and mind raging unlike any war the world had ever known.

The only reason she had managed time tonight was because Gilles had gone out after supper and said he would not be back before dawn. She hadn't asked any questions, and neither Mrs. Corbin nor the other servants seemed to think anything was amiss by his going.

It was now or never.

Abby walked unsteadily towards the servants' wing of the house, her legs still not where she would have liked them to be after her adventure in the caves. Instead of the shuffle-and-clunk gait she was used to, she now had a creaky and steady dragging one, and her bad knee shook if she put too much pressure on it. She'd fallen yesterday, but only enough to bruise her pride. No one had seen, and she had conveniently avoided telling anyone about it.

She would continue to heal and strengthen, of course. She simply needed the time to do so. And she was *not* about to spend more time in her bed, being doted on by people with better things to do.

Once she reached this older part of the house, Abby began to look at everything more carefully. Any painting out of place could indicate a secret door. Any rug that did not belong could hide a trap door. Any corridor could lead somewhere important.

She inhaled slowly, closing her eyes for a moment, held her breath for a few heartbeats, then exhaled a steady, almost silent stream of air. She could feel the training she'd received and given carefully snap into place in her mind, sending a wave of calm into her body and filling her thoughts with clarity and alertness.

Sage might be retired and gone, but Pearl was here.

And no one would know what to expect from Pearl.

Not even Pearl.

She opened her eyes and began to move again, her eyes tracking everything and anything about her surroundings. Her mind filled with insights and details, filtering them one after the other with ease and sorting them into categories. Important, interesting, and irrelevant, for a start, though she could go back and think on them all again later and restructure. The amount of information she'd have to find tonight was too much for a thorough evaluation on sight, so her training in memorization and recall would come into play.

The trouble was that everything seemed to be fairly open in this part of the house. No doors were locked, artwork was minimal, and there were absolutely no rugs. It was almost as though they were trying to show there was nothing to hide back here, which was even more bewildering.

Abby wandered through the kitchens, examining every detail and every floorboard, but still found nothing. Even the larder held no clues or secrets, and she'd pressed on enough bricks to give her a fairly good indication of any hidden passages or doors. But still, the memory of the cave and its depth ate at her, warning her of something. Teasing her, in a way, and she did not believe in coincidences. If something bothered her, instinct was telling her something.

But what?

She stood in the servants' dining room, a rather cavernous space that led out into the courtyard by way of a few steps, given the sunken nature of this portion of the house. She had stepped on each and every stone in this room, studied every nook and cranny, and there was nothing out of the ordinary or in any way suspicious. The complete lack of anything was suspicious, but how could she send that information out?

I haven't found anything, and that is suspicious. Please advise.

She snorted softly to herself, shaking her head. Milliner would be annoyed at the waste of parchment for such a message, if nothing else. Operatives were trained to think for themselves, not to be guided by someone at every point. She had to figure this out on her own, and she had certainly gotten information out of more complicated places.

Just not any that meant as much to her.

Her eyes fell on the courtyard just beyond, and she moved in that direction, tilting her head as her heart began to pound a little harder. It was the middle of the night, but her eyes had so adjusted to the dark of the house that being outside was actually brighter for the moment. Slowly, she walked around the courtyard, sweeping her eyes from left to right in an easy motion, almost as though she were looking for a lost piece of jewelry amid the stones.

She'd never been out here before; there had never been a reason to. The family didn't use the courtyard for anything; only deliveries to the house and preparations of horses and carriages were done back here. The space was tidy and well kept, and remnants of a fountain sat in the middle of it, but it was clear that had been gone for some time.

Her eyes fell to the ground around the base where the fountain had once been. Where there had been water, there just might be…

Abby bit the inside of her lip and began slowly walking around the base, her pulse thundering in her ears and drowning out the sounds of the night and her own breathing. There would be something here, she could feel it. Sense it.

There.

An old, rusted iron loop sat almost flush with the ground against the ancient stone base, barely big enough for two fingers to hook into. She stooped quickly and pulled at it, feeling only the slightest bit of give. Whatever door it opened would be heavy, but if she could find a way to ease its opening…

Abby went to her knees and traced her fingers on the ground just in front of the loop, finding a small crevice her eyes had missed. She ran a finger along the crevice, no matter where it went, taking care to avoid believing a space between stone could be it. She could feel dust and powder collecting on her finger and into her nail as she traced, but she didn't care. Finding this space would be worth any disgust or discomfort.

After a few minutes, she had the general idea of this trap door of sorts, and she shifted into a better position for leverage and hooked her fingers into the loop once more. Bracing her feet against the stone, she heaved with all of her might, and felt the stone shift. She hissed between her teeth and continued to pull, the groaning of the stone rumbling in her ears. If it wouldn't give more than this, she was going to wake someone.

The resistance against her arms faded as the door broke the surface of the ground, and Abby gasped in relief. Holding it open by the loop, she moved to the side and gripped the thick side of the door, heaving it the rest of the way open. It rested against the surrounding stone easily, and once she was certain it would not close unexpectedly, Abby moved to look into the opening.

It was perfectly dark, and there was no sign of how to get down there.

She frowned, glancing around, and smirked when she caught sight of lanterns against the wall. She hurried over and grabbed one before moving back into the kitchen, where the coals from the night's supper still glowed in places. She pulled the candle out of the lantern and teased the wick until it stood perfectly upright, then touched it to the brightest coal she could find.

It took a moment or two, but then the wick caught, and a feeble flame began to flicker. She replaced it in the lantern and closed the door, moving back out to the courtyard quickly. Lying on the ground, she reached the lantern as far down into the darkness as possible, her eyes squinting to see whatever was there.

A ladder extended up to the door, which answered that question, but the space below was what caught her interest. It was a large room, the walls entirely stone and resembling the cave walls. There were four cots to one side and two desks to another. A shelf scattered with books leaned against one wall, and the other…

The other held an opening that moved off in the direction of the caves.

Abby scooted closer to the opening until her head was over it entirely, and turned her ear towards the darkness, closing her eyes and focusing all of her attention on what she could hear.

For a long moment, there was nothing. But then…

Drip. Drip. Drip-drop. Drip.

There it was. She couldn't be entirely certain, of course, without venturing within and tracing everything by foot, but she was confident enough to suspect this room led to that open space beyond the third cave, where she hadn't been able to go.

So what was this space used for? Who was landing at the Coutanche beaches and staying in this room beneath the ground where no one would find them? Based on the effort she had to put in to get the door open, she could presume it hadn't been used for some time, but it had been used at some point, and conditions within seemed fair enough that it could be used again at any time.

Abby moved herself back from the hole and set the lantern aside before going to the door and carefully, quietly, closing it all back up. There were still the telltale scraping sounds of stone against stone, but it was softer than the groans that had come when she opened it. She blew out the lantern and placed it back with the others, then slipped back into the house, walking back towards the main portion with as much haste as her gait would allow her.

She needed to get back into Gilles's study. She might find a decent explanation for the who and where and how of the room, and if she knew that, the letters she could intercept might allow her to interrupt the next…

The possibilities were beginning to open up, and she had to force her heart to stop its fierce burning and pounding, convinced she would wake up tomorrow with bruises around her ribs from its activity.

She felt as though she barely took a breath as she made her way to the study. Her legs forgot to shake when she walked, and her hands almost itched with the desire to run over surfaces to find more abnormalities and insights. She couldn't recollect when she had last felt this connected to her operative side, but it was as freeing as the moment she'd had in the warm pool, only more satisfying.

This, at least, hadn't gone anywhere she could not retrieve it.

The study door opened with just as much silence as before and the room appeared just as she had left it the last time she had entered.

This time, she had no hesitation. She moved to the windows and yanked the curtains open for each one, letting the moonlight and starlight stream into the space. Then she turned and looked at the entire room with an awake and discerning eye.

What had she missed the last time she was in here? There had to be more, and now that she knew Gilles even better…

Gilles.

Her heart sprang into her throat, fairly choking her with the betrayal in which she was currently engaged. He would never forgive her when all of this was over.

Which was why operatives should never get emotionally attached in the first place, but as it was…

Her eyes narrowed. What did she know about Gilles that could give her insight in this room? She let her gaze trace up and down the bookshelves, the desk, the chair, the floor…

A simple and soft rug lay across the floor in front of his desk, only visible from this side at the moment, given her position. But it was a very light cream color, and nothing else in the space was so fair a shade. And why would it need to be soft? This was a study, not a bedchamber.

In fact, the rug could have been made from the wool of a sheep, based on its appearance.

Sheep.

Eyes widening, Abby took two steps forward and dropped to the floor just in front of the rug. *The Odyssey.* His favorite book. And the sheep escaping from the cave…

She flung the rug back, revealing a small, tidy trap door. This one had a hook that was flush with the floor, allowing the rug to lay perfectly flat and give nothing away.

Opening the door, Abby sat back on her heels, willing her chest to loosen in its present torment of her heart and lungs. She reached into the space, finding several folded pieces of parchment, ledgers, and journals. She pulled everything out she could, including a signet ring, of all things.

She went to the papers first, finding both letters in French and English, none of which had any specific significance within. But then there were other loose pieces, and those had quite a bit of information in them, and one word in particular caught her eye.

Allred.

"Oh, dear Lord, no," she breathed, the words catching painfully in her throat. She scanned the lines three times, but there was no mistaking it. Allred. Bride. Warehouse.

Abby closed her eyes as a wash of nausea cascaded through her, creating a faint shudder that left her colder than any flooding cave ever could.

How could Gilles be involved with this? *How?* The Faction was one thing, but kidnapping innocent girls to have them married off to Faction members for their connection to Society? It went against everything that Gilles had shown himself to be to her, and everything he would want for his daughters. How could he hide that part of himself so well that she couldn't even spot hints of it?

She was a covert operative, for heaven's sake! She had been trained to notice everything about people and how to spot lies within moments in any given conversation. But she hadn't seen or felt anything deceptive in Gilles. Those instincts did not vanish so easily, especially when she was regularly teaching new operatives the very same thing at the Convent. These skills were always in use for her. Always.

Which meant… she couldn't be wrong. Not entirely.

But then what was all this? What was Gilles doing, and what could any of this mean?

She set the letters aside and picked up the ledgers, thumbing through the first of them quickly. They bore the same sort of details that the book in his desk had. Only numbers, checks, and circles. No words whatsoever.

The next had words and numbers, but the words didn't form any sort of context. *Candle, India, Apple, Cheese, Arrow, Rain…* Completely nonsensical, and yet they had to mean something to someone, or they wouldn't have had a line in the ledger.

Another ledger had more numbers, but no checks or circles.

It was maddening to see a wealth of information that meant absolutely nothing to her. And when she came across another ledger with random words and numbers, she gave up, closing it and stacking it with the others. She leaned forward and gripped at her hair, growling softly to herself.

Something was right in front of her face, and she wasn't seeing it. Something was missing.

She straightened and looked through the journals, all written in French and dated. From quick reading, it seemed as though it was a record of letters sent and received, but she would have to go through letter by letter to be sure. There was no time for that, and there were far more entries in the journals than there were letters in the space. Dates went back more than five years, and that was terrifying.

What if he'd known about the assignment where her injury had occurred?

Her injury had nothing to do with that assignment, of course. Yes, her body had already been in a weakened state, which was from the assignment, but the damage itself was pure accident and coincidence. Yet it somehow was crushing to think that Gilles might have passed a message to someone about the very assignment where her life had shifted forever.

Abby exhaled slowly, shaking her head as she set the journals to one side and picked up the signet ring, turning it towards the window for better lighting. There was an anchor in the center, but around the edges were the words *Un lointain rivage.*

Foreign shore.

Exactly like the cufflink Sparrow had found in the cave at Barcliffe on her assignment.

Worse and worse.

She ran her finger over the surface of the ring, barely even feeling the engravings etched in it. The ridges were so smooth now, the details so buffered by use that the seal must be faint in any wax. How many Faction letters had this ring sealed so far?

How many more would it seal?

The door to the study burst open then, startling a yelp from her throat, and she looked up in horror.

Gilles stood in the doorway, lit candelabra in hand. His brows were raised as he took in her position, the rug, the items around her…

Abby couldn't breathe. Couldn't swallow. Couldn't move.

Couldn't.

Slowly, Gilles entered the room and closed the door behind him, turning the key into the lock. He turned and faced her, leaning his back against the door as he stared at her, his expression bordering on the dangerous.

"I think, Abigail, it is time to tell me who you really are."

Chapter Fourteen

Zut. Zut. Zut.

And damn it all to hell at that.

Nothing could have prepared Gilles for the sight of Abigail sitting on the floor of his study, rifling through the contents of his secret compartment, his entire operative life on full display. The fear in her eyes, as well as the comprehension, told him that her being here was no accident. That she had known to look for something. That she'd had an ulterior motive for being here.

That, somewhere, lies had been spoken.

He ought to have been furious. He ought to have raged. He ought to have felt or said or done any number of things at being discovered in such a way, especially by the woman he loved. By being betrayed, in a way, by the same.

But instead, he felt remarkably calm. His mind raced, of course, but his heart did not.

He knew Abigail. Or whatever her name was. He'd known enough liars and actors in his life to tell the difference between what was genuine and what was not, and everything about Abigail screamed genuine from head to toe. Whatever lies existed had to be minimal at best, else he would have to call himself gullible and blind.

He had never been either, and he was not about to begin now.

Abigail still sat on the floor staring at him, her fingers clutching at the signet ring.

She looked utterly terrified.

He hated that.

Sighing, Gilles set the candelabra on the floor, then sank onto it himself, leaning against the door. He rested his arms on the tops of his knees and tilted his head back to rest against the door as well. It was as casual a position as he could think of under the circumstances.

"Abigail," he said simply, not bothering to smile, as he wasn't sure how she would take it. "Please."

She blinked almost owlishly at him, then slowly lowered the ring to her lap. Her eyes never left his, and just as before, he felt as though she could see directly into his soul. Only there was no heat to be found in it now, only worry.

"Am I going to get hurt?" she whispered.

His heart seemed to crack in his chest, and he heard it do so. "Abigail…"

"Will you let me leave after I tell you everything?"

Ice raced through his veins and his breath caught painfully in his throat. "Leave?"

"Leave," she said again. "You won't want me here once you know, I can promise you that."

Oh, how little she knew him!

Now he did smile, chuckling very softly. "You cannot, in fact, promise me that, but if it will make you feel better… When you have told me who you are and what you know, you may go as freely as you came. But as a courtesy, I will tell you now that you do not know nearly as much as you think you do, and you have as little reason to fear me as you do a spaniel."

Her brow creased rather impressively at his words, her lips pursing.

Gilles had to grin at the sight. Either she was from the Faction, or she was from the English, and he could play this either way. He'd have a much harder time if she was from the Faction, but if she was from the English operatives, his life was about to improve exponentially.

But he would not deny that it was a complicated, confusing situation for someone to come into with only half of the information. It was confusing enough with both sides.

"I am trusting you, Gilles," Abigail murmured in a low, throaty voice that made him burn as much as it made him sad. "I hope I am not doing so in vain."

"You're not," he whispered back, nodding his encouragement.

She did not return it. Her eyes lowered to the overturned portion of the rug, and he heard her soft exhale. "My name is Abigail Charteris. I have been an operative in the service of England since I was eighteen years of age."

Gilles let his eyelids flutter a touch in relief, a silent exhale making his body almost weak.

"I have been teaching for five years at Miss Masters's School for Fine Young Ladies in Kent," Abigail went on, her voice never wavering. "My assignment was to come here and investigate you as a member of the French Faction that supports the ideals of Sieyès and wishes to take down the French government, the British crown, and various corners of Europe."

Well, that summed it up nicely, didn't it? The Faction wanted a great deal more than that, but he would let that be for now.

Abigail cleared her throat and straightened where she sat. "You came to our attention after a foiled kidnapping of a young lady in London. Lucy Allred."

Gilles felt his smile evaporate and his hands began to tighten into fists. Allred?

"Her father had a part in it." Abigail swallowed quickly, her eyes still on the floor. "He told operatives that someone approached him and offered to satisfy his extensive debts if his daughter was given to a man named Bichard, who wanted to enter London Society but had no connections."

"*Zut alors!*" Gilles pushed to his feet in one swift movement and grabbed the candelabra, racing to his desk.

Abigail fell backwards in alarm, but clambered to her feet. "Gilles? Gilles, I told you it was a foiled attempt. We stopped it."

"They're going for it again," he ground out, yanking out his drawer and pulling another piece of parchment out. "I don't have time to explain everything, *ma douce,* but believe me, I want exactly what you want at this point."

"So it's not you who wants to go into London Society?"

He snorted loudly as he scribbled out the message he wished to send. "*Absolument pas,*" he grunted. "Why do you think I live on Guernsey? But I won't have a choice now. My idiot *gaspilleur* of a brother burns with the passion of *l'Faction* and is blind to their evils. I have no doubt he is the one they wish to have enter English Society, even at the expense of an innocent young woman."

"What do you mean you'll have no choice?" Abigail snapped as she looked at what he was writing.

"I will have to offer myself to go to London," he said shortly as he began to transcribe his words into code on a separate sheet. "I already have connections through my wife's family, so it would negate the need for a bride for anyone. If I had known this was what they meant, I would have done it months ago, but *évidemment* no one wishes to speak clearly, even in their messages to each other."

Abigail was silent as he worked through the code he'd had memorized for so long, he no longer needed the rubric to guide his actions.

"You intercept letters," she finally stated, her voice barely audible over the scratching of his quill. "Faction letters."

"Oui," he quipped, his attention on the code still. "But that is my task, *ma douce*. It is easier to get letters to our members through me than general post. I send all of them to one person, and he has his own riders go out with them. One in England, one in France. But they don't know that I open and decipher everything and also send anything of interest or import to my other contacts in England."

Her hand fell on his arm, pausing his writing. "Other contacts?"

Gilles looked up and met her eyes, so brilliant and richly blue even in this dim light. And so perfectly filled with hope at this moment that he could not resist leaning in and kissing her fiercely, nipping at her lips just once.

"Oui, ma douce," he whispered, reaching up to brush her bottom lip with his thumb. "Perhaps you know them. Trick, for one."

Her eyes went perfectly round at that. "You know Trick?"

He grinned and kissed her quickly before returning to his coding. "Only by my pen. He calls me Briton, which I find shockingly apt. He also has me write to Iris, but she is less fun to correspond with."

"Iris?"

"And there was some contact with Trace before his unfortunate presumed death," Gilles said with a sigh, as though only recollecting in passing. "But that was mostly Heloise and her sister."

"What?"

Chuckling, Gilles glanced at Abigail for one brief moment. *"Ma douce,* there is much to discuss, but if we wish to prevent any more trouble…" He gestured to his letter.

That snapped her out of her stupor, and she reached over him to grab a piece of parchment for herself. "Right. I'll write to my superior as well and let her know of the situation. Do Trick and Iris know of the continuing plot?"

"I assume so, given what I have told them and what you have told me." He scribbled a few more words and signed the note before grabbing a bit of pounce to set the ink. "Allred is missing, but they are looking for him. I now presume your people have him safely stowed somewhere. They are looking for new brides, have settled between two, and another warehouse has been secured, likely to be used as a rendezvous location." He barked a cold laugh. "And here I was concerned about an elopement needing to use Coutanche as a safe haven."

Abigail hummed a sound of disapproval as she scratched out her own missive. "Only partially wrong, I suppose. Would your brother really show up here with his kidnapped bride in tow?"

Gilles frowned at that, thinking a moment. *"Non,* Gaston would never get his own hands dirty. And I have no reason to believe he has ever been to London, so whoever is assigned to fetch the girl would bring her here, and he would follow another time. Who knows what lies they would have told me?"

"I found your secret room in the caves," Abigail told him as she reached over him for the pounce to dry her own missive. "Would they have stayed there?"

He looked at her in delighted pride. "You certainly did the thing properly, didn't you, *ma douce?"* He chuckled, shaking his head as he folded his letter and began melting the wax for a seal. *"Non,* the only ones who stay in there are the operatives either fleeing England or sneaking into it. We haven't had them for a few years now, but recent letters indicated I might be used again. But did anybody tell me that directly? *Non. Des secrets exaspérants."*

He pressed the wax against the parchment and picked up the signet ring Abigail had set on the desk, sealing the wax firmly with it.

Abigail used the same wax to seal her letter, then wiped her hands on her skirts, exhaling slowly. "How do we get these out quickly, Gilles?"

"I'll send a rider to my contact at the docks. He can get them to England well before nightfall tomorrow."

"Even mine?"

Gilles turned to her and put both hands on her upper arms, rubbing gently. "Even yours, Abigail. He is not a member of *l'Faction*, only a man I pay very well to take my letters where they need to go. He will see them both delivered with equal haste. Do you trust me?"

Her eyes searched his a moment, but the answer was already there in her gaze. "Yes."

He leaned in and pressed his lips to her brow gently, breathing in her essence and her goodness. "Thank you, *ma douce.*" He pulled back and stroked her cheek, then held out his hand for her letter. "May I?"

She handed it over, and he picked up his own letter as well, slapping both into the palm of his hand. "I will be back very soon. Please, don't leave. There is more to say, I think."

Abigail swallowed and nodded, stepping back from the desk. "Yes, there is. Hurry."

He smiled tightly and gripped her hand before moving out of the room, striding down the corridor at a clip.

He hadn't thought to return to Coutanche before morning, but taking a number of letters to Allaire hadn't taken as long as he'd thought, and he hadn't bothered to spend any time down in the village. At this time of night, all he could do was take lodgings at the local inn, but his own bed and his own home had called to him instead. What might have gone on if he hadn't arrived at that precise moment? He might never have known who Abigail was, and they might not have realized the gravity of the situation taking place in England.

Now he had to try and get these letters to accompany the others before the ship to Poole left. It ought to be fine, given the usual time of departure, but nevertheless…

The gamekeeper's cottage was just a short walk from the main house, so Gilles was there and pounding on the door before his thoughts could venture too far into worrying.

It took several rounds of pounding before the door opened, and Simms squinted at him, bleary-eyed even in the dark of the night. "Mr. Bichard?"

"Excuses, Simms, but I need you to ride these down to Allaire at this moment. They must sail with him on the morning tide." He handed the letters over, as well as a pouch of coins. "This plus the same again if he can get these delivered before what he already has. Can you do it?"

Simms rubbed a hand over his face, blinking several times as he nodded. "Yes, sir. Of course, sir. I'll go now."

Gilles nodded and clapped him on the shoulder. "I'll see a horse saddled for you now. *Merci, mon ami."* He turned and headed for the stables, not bothering to wake anyone as he got one of the horses readied for the venture. Why wake more of his staff than he needed to? Besides, he preferred to saddle the horse himself when he rode anyway, so he was perfectly practiced in it.

Simms was at the stables just a few moments later, looking at him with surprise. "I could have done that, sir."

"I know, but now you don't have to." Gilles rubbed the horse's nose gently and led him out, handing the reins to Simms, who nodded. "Godspeed."

He didn't wait for Simms to leave before returning to the house, flexing his fingers a few times as he walked.

Everything was out of his hands and his control at the moment. He had done all he could once the information was his, and all he could do now was wait. They might not take him up on his offer, but if they were wise, they would see the sense in it. There would be less trouble to stir up if he was the man they chose to enter London Society.

He groaned at the very idea of London, and what it would mean, but if it would spare some girl from being forced to marry his brother, he could breathe a little easier about it.

Making his way back to the study, Gilles felt the weight of what he had just taken on, what had been revealed, and the sheer lateness of the hour. His body was exhausted, but his mind whirled and clicked like some obscure contraption with far too many mechanisms and no real purpose. Everything was going to change for him and for his daughters, and their idyllic life on Guernsey, away from the trouble of the Faction, would be over.

He would be stepping into the lion's den without any certainty he would be delivered.

Abigail stood by the windows of his study, looking out at the distant sea, but she turned as he closed the door. "I saw Simms ride off. Will he make it?"

"I believe so," Gilles murmured, rubbing a hand through his hair. "Allaire sails on the morning tide, but that's a relative term, in his mind. He's never failed me before."

She nodded softly and leaned back against the windows, staring at him. "Can we talk?"

He gave her a tired smile and went over to the desk, but instead of sitting there, sat himself on the floor by the windows and leaned against the wall. "By all means. Let's talk."

If she was surprised by his position, she made no sign of it. Instead, she lowered herself to the floor and mirrored him, laying her head against the wall to stare directly at him.

He stared right back, smiling at the feeling of a striking blow to his gut that filled the space with heat. "The way you stare, Abigail…" He shook his head. "I'll never grow accustomed to it."

"I don't mean to," she murmured. "I mean, I don't intend for anyone to be affected by my looking at them."

"Then you don't see yourself very well." He chuckled softly. "I would wager people tell you everything. Reveal their entire souls and all their secrets."

Her lips curved in a small smile. "Not quite, but they do tell me quite a bit, it seems."

He rolled his hand and wrist in a bit of a flourish before gesturing at her, winking at her grin. "Your power, *ma douce.*"

"You still call me that," Abigail said in a low voice, the words tinged with wonder. "After what I've told you, you still…"

"What has changed?" he overrode gently, shrugging. "Your surname. Your reason for coming here, perhaps. But you are the same. Your ability to teach and charm my daughters has not changed. Your sincere affection towards them has not changed. Your heart has not changed. Your beauty has not changed. Your spirit has not changed. Therefore, the way I feel for you has not changed."

Her eyes shimmered in the flickering candlelight. "How?" she asked hoarsely. "How can you feel that way? I… betrayed you."

Gilles cocked his head slightly, heat pulsing through his frame. "Did you? Did you really?"

"I came here to investigate you," she choked out, swiping at falling tears.

"Did you have feelings for me when you took the assignment?"

She coughed a watery laugh. "No, of course not."

"Then you were simply fulfilling your assignment, which shows honor and integrity." He shouldn't be enjoying this, but God help him, he was. He was loving that he could help her see how he felt about her at the same time as learn more about her feelings, and all secrets between them would be laid to rest.

Well, what secrets that had no impact on national security, of course.

He'd allow those.

Abigail hiccupped on more tears, cursing to herself as she wiped her cheeks again. "But after we… once we… I still did it. I invaded your study and found your work."

"Because you are a skilled operative," he said simply. "I commend you. I should have hidden it better. How did you know to find it?"

She waved her hand at the rug as her throat bobbed on a swallow. "The rug looks like sheep's wool, and I remembered you love *The Odyssey.*"

"*Tres bien, ma douce,*" Gilles praised with a laugh, dropping his head back against the wall. "I believe it is safe to say that not many others would have made that conclusion."

"Gilles! How are you not furious?" she demanded, her hands making some sort of slapping sound.

He looked at her and saw her palms flat against her thighs, her eyes full of confusion now. He softened and smiled as gently as he could. "Because, *ma douce,* we are on the same side. And I am not angry because I know your heart. I could feel it, *vous comprenez?* From the very first moment. So I knew that whoever you were, whatever you were doing, your intentions were pure, and I could trust them."

She shook her head slowly, looking as though she might crumple where she sat.

He wanted nothing more than to take her into his arms, but he sensed there was something that needed to be closed between them first. Something that needed to be said, acknowledged, or done, and until it was, nothing would truly be settled.

"*Ma douce,*" he began slowly, "did you believe I was a villain? Not when you took the assignment, but once you were here."

The muscles in her throat flickered with tension, and she shook her head. "No. No, I… I've never believed that. It's why I've had so little to report back. I've found nothing, and I didn't… I didn't want to find anything. I couldn't believe that you would ever do what I was supposed to think you had. I could not reconcile the man I knew with the one I was supposed to investigate. I've never wanted to fail in a mission before in my entire life."

"You saw me," Gilles murmured, his voice fairly rumbling from his chest as it reached across the room for her. "I'd hoped you would."

She nodded at him, and he saw the renewed moisture in her eyes, her lower lip quivering.

His throat constricted, and he held a hand out to her. "*Viens ici, ma douce.*"

Abigail crawled over to him and immediately snuggled up to his side, her head resting on his chest as her tears fell against him. He wrapped her in his arms and let his fingers thread through her hair as he kissed her brow repeatedly. Soft, grazing kisses meant to comfort and console as well as convey.

He sighed as he rested his chin against her head, rocking just a little. "I joined *l'Faction* at age twenty, and Gaston followed suit. We joined for France and for the chance to restore her to glory after *la Révolution* and Napoleon brought us down. I never cared about the aristocracy or the monarchy, just France. I did not see a reason for so much bloodshed to have taken place then, but I have never lived in Paris. I was just a boy in Quimper. What did I know about such things? And Napoleon…"

He scoffed loudly, shaking his head. "Arrogant fool. Whatever his initial plans, he made a mess of everything else. We only wanted to do better by France and for France. I met Heloise at a gathering in Orléans that was intended to be a recruiting mission. I think the only person I recruited was her, and that was a triumph enough for me."

Abigail snickered softly, nuzzling against him as her arms wrapped around his waist.

Gilles closed his eyes in memory, and in delight at having her in his hold. "We married straightaway. Too quickly for some, but we knew our minds. We settled in Brittany thereafter, and I continued to work for *l'Faction* however I could. But Heloise… she had clearer vision than I did. Her father was British and had come to France as an operative himself, not that she told me that right away. But she could see the warning signs early and acted accordingly. She began to take my messages and send the information to England without my knowledge."

Abigail stilled against him, and he could feel how her heart pounded.

"Her older half-sister has been involved with several operatives and assignments over the years," Gilles went on, continuing his almost hypnotic motion of running his fingers through her long tresses. "The two of them worked out a coded system for themselves and she connected Heloise with the right individuals to receive information. That is how the figure of Briton was born. It was Heloise, until I started to express my doubts and fears to her about what *l'Faction* was becoming."

He laughed a little as he pulled back and looked Abigail in the eyes. "You should have seen my reaction to her confession then, *ma douce*. Anger became disbelief, which became pride and relief. She saw me as well, and knew I would want to help. So from then on, we became Briton. I stayed within the ranks to continue the flow of information, and we ensured that England got what was relevant."

"And Gaston?" she asked, her eyes flicking between his.

Gilles sighed heavily, shaking his head. "We grew apart. He does not know of my disenchantment, but he does know I do not possess the same passion for the cause as he does. He attributes this to my marriage and children, but it has always been this way. He, on the other hand… He will do anything to rise in the ranks."

"Like take part in an abduction plot for a connected English wife," Abigail said quietly, shaking her head.

"I still cannot believe they have done this," Gilles growled, dropping his head back against the wall again. "Have they lost all sense of themselves? Forcing a young woman to act a part for her entire marriage when she is a prisoner… That is cruel, and they would be condemning her to no end of abuse within the privacy of her marriage. Especially if she weds Gaston and does not share his devotion to the cause."

He closed his eyes, exhaling slowly. "I do not want to move to London, and I do not want to move the girls to London."

He felt Abigail sit up and let his arm go loose about her shoulders. "Then why offer yourself? You could stay out of it entirely, Gilles. Leave foiling the abductions to us."

His eyes snapped open as he stared at her, irritation flaring at her for the very first time. "You really believe I could stand by and let that happen? Risk what happened to Mademoiselle Allred happening to someone else? Even if you can stop a dozen abductions, Abigail, it will not be enough. No father should feel as though he should sell his daughter, and no daughter should be used as a pawn in some stupid game of men. How can I stay out of this when I am a perfect solution to end it?"

Abigail smiled at him then, so tenderly and so gently that his breath caught in his chest, trapped and flailing against several ribs. She laid her hand along his cheek, stroking softly. "You're Odysseus, aren't you? The cursed warrior trying to get home and doing everything in his power to see right restored."

Gilles managed a weak laugh. "Perhaps. But that would make France my Penelope, and her suitors this group of men who have distorted everything."

Her smile turned a trifle wry, but her hand did not move. "What would you do when you're back with Penelope, then? In this Odysseus world you've imagined."

"Rule Ithaca, of course."

"Which is?"

"My life." He shrugged a shoulder. "Or my happiness, perhaps."

Abigail's brows knitted together. "But can you not be happy

without her?"

He leaned into her touch, and began running his fingers along the back of her hand and to her wrist. "Certainly. Just not to the fullest extent. And that is not to say that I have to be in France once it is restored. Only that it is restored. That will be enough."

"Why is that an important distinction?"

He kissed the palm of her hand and sat forward, taking her face in both of his hands and meeting her gaze with all of the raw intensity he could muster. "Because I don't want you to believe that one day I must return to France in order to be my happiest. I want my life to be with you, Abigail. As much as I want France restored. I will never be fully happy without you either. And I will live anywhere in this world in utter bliss if you are with me."

Her mouth fell open as she stared at him, completely devoid of sound.

Gilles ran his thumb along her bottom lip gently. "I love you, Abigail Charteris."

She closed her mouth, clamping down on her lips hard before shaking her head quickly. "I love you," she gasped, closing the distance between them and slamming her lips to his.

He cradled her as she came flush against him, her arms folding about his neck as though determined to rid any distance at all between this embrace. Her very soul was in her endless, ravenous kiss, and he took every bit of it and gave his own. There was too much and yet not enough, no sating the hunger that was building and yet fulfilling every wish he'd ever had. Breathless and starving, yet renewed and whole.

Home.

Wherever she was, he would be home.

Epilogue

"Gilles, you are driving me insane! Why won't you tell me who she is?"

"Because, *ma douce,* it is that secret. Now that I'm in London, and you've agreed to marry me, she will become even more important."

Abby frowned at her intended as they walked into the unfamiliar townhouse. It was clear he was not about to budge on this, but it had been days of this merciless secret keeping, and she was beyond irritated now.

No one had told her whose house this was, why this had to be such a private gathering, or why the coach had taken at least seven unnecessary turns in bringing them here. She was a covert operative, for heaven's sake, and even she had never employed these extensive tactics. Was this mysterious half-sister of his late wife actually one of the king's sisters? There was no other possibility with all of this being implemented.

The last month had been an absolute whirlwind, and being in London for a week hadn't done anything to lessen it.

The Faction had accepted Gilles's offer to be their fresh contact in London Society, and they'd asked him to be there as soon as possible. He'd been in endless meetings with known Faction members and supporters, leaving him in no doubt of what his role would be and how crucial it was to them.

It would make his task of deception and interception more difficult, but he was willing.

Gaston was no longer going to take an unwilling Society bride, but as the orders had come from those he respected, the decision was accepted easily. Whether that would help the brothers gain any sort of relationship akin to the one they had lost was in doubt, but Gilles did not seem particularly concerned about that.

Abby, for one, hadn't expected to come away from her assignment with an engagement, but there was nothing to be done about it now. She'd met with Milliner first thing, and after loudly expressing concerns that all of her teachers were going to leave her to become wives and mothers, they'd begun to strategize how to best use her in the new position she would take up.

Gilles, on the other hand, had finally met Trick in person, but refused to tell Abby who else had been there. It would be better, for now, if their contacts were fairly separate so as to eliminate confusion. They would only work together as Briton when the time called for it, and she would still be Pearl in the meanwhile. They could confide in each other and advise and such, but their assignments would be separate.

Mostly.

When she was Mrs. Bichard, she would be attending all of the same Society functions he would, including meeting with all of his old and new associates. She would have to be charming and graceful, filled with politeness and natural disinterest towards anything of a political nature, and familiar with everyone and everything Society had to offer.

It would be the role of a lifetime, and she was eager to get started.

Not least because she would be Mrs. Bichard in truth, which was all she really wanted.

He offered her a home for life with his love, and she was clinging to that for all it was worth.

The girls had no real qualms about leaving Guernsey for London, especially with the understanding that they would be going back from time to time, particularly when the numbers in Society were depleted.

Apparently, the Faction still loved that Gilles had a home with a beachside cavernous access, so they wanted him there occasionally.

Gilles had found it very interesting that he was now so important when he had been merely the manager of the post for the last few years.

Abby did not find it interesting. She saw the wisdom in it at once. Gilles was throwing himself into the heart of Faction operations, which would show interest and loyalty. They were rewarding him with their attention and using what he had to offer.

It meant he would gain even more information and insight into future plans and operations, which would be turned over to the English operatives and the Shopkeepers for their use.

This was going to be a brilliant excursion, however long it lasted.

He did have the assurance of his superiors that he would not be in any actual danger, as he had daughters to think of, and he was holding them to that assurance.

Whether or not it was true would remain to be seen.

"Abigail. Come along."

Abby started, not realizing she had paused her step in her reflection and hurried up to Gilles, taking his hand in hers and lacing their fingers. "What is she going to think of me?"

He looked surprised by the question. "I never took you for an insecure creature, my Abigail. What's brought this on?"

"I'm meeting the English half-sister of your late wife," she bit out a bit more harshly than she intended, her chest tightening with nerves. "It's practically like meeting Heloise herself while knowing I am stepping into her place as your wife and the maternal figure of your daughters! Who wouldn't have insecurities about this?"

"Shh, *ma douce,*" Gilles soothed, taking her hand and kissing the back twice before kissing the palm. "My goodness, I had no idea you felt this way."

Abby wasn't entirely certain she wanted him knowing she felt this way, but anxieties were what they were, and they'd just come barreling out of her like she had no control whatsoever. Her cheeks began to heat as mortification slipped in and she closed her eyes, swallowing hard.

She felt his gentle touch on her cheek and knew he wanted her eyes, so she opened them and looked at him in spite of everything.

His smile was just as warm and delightful as it had ever been, his eyes crinkling beautifully. "Heloise would have adored you. The two of you would have been fast friends and left me out of everything. Her sister is much like her, in her own way, and will bear you no ill will or even judgment for marrying me. Well, perhaps judgment, because I fully believe she will be of the opinion that you deserve better, but there is no accounting for taste."

Abby giggled as the man she adored made a sympathetic face. How did he manage to amuse and settle her in one single breath? How could he know exactly what she needed and give it so freely?

How had she ever lived her life without him?

She looped her arms around his neck, sighing softly. "I love you."

Gilles leaned in and kissed her slowly, but thoroughly. "I love you, too, Abigail." He brushed his nose against hers and took her hand again, winking as their fingers naturally folded together. "Come."

With a gentle tug, he pulled her down the marble corridor and to a room on the right at the end of it, a quiet, yellow-papered drawing room.

It was empty.

"I thought we might be first," Gilles said as they entered. "We will only have a few moments to wait." He walked over to the divan closest to the window and sat, looking around the room almost fondly.

Abby watched him, puzzled. "Have you been here before?"

"Once," he replied easily. "After I married Heloise. It is the home of her godfather."

"Who is?"

"Dead."

Abby rolled her eyes, shaking her head and walking to the windows. "You cannot even tell me that much?"

"I would apologize, *ma douce,* but I was sworn to absolute secrecy. It is your country's protectors who have insisted it, so what can I do?" He only shrugged, completely unruffled by any of this.

Truth be told, Abby wasn't all that upset either. Whoever was managing all of this would have had their reasons, and if Heloise was that well connected, it would be crucial indeed to protect it. One could only imagine who her father must have been as an operative and as a man. Some influence, if not fortune as well, and certainly plenty of training.

A family tradition that might be continuing, it seemed.

"So you said this sister helped Heloise to assume her role of Briton?" Abby eventually said when the silence became too much.

"*Oui.* They corresponded regularly, albeit complicatedly."

Abby blinked and turned to face him. "Is that even a word?"

Gilles laughed loudly once. "*Je ne sais pas, ma douce.* It is your language, not mine."

"How was it complicated?" she asked, folding her arms.

"They wrote in code, and the letters had to be sent to a contact in Paris, who would then send it to whichever sister it was for." Gilles shook his head, still laughing. "It took twice as long to get anywhere, but they insisted on it."

Abby scoffed, unable to believe the lengths they went to. "Whatever for?"

"Because no one could know we were sisters. Heloise would never have been trusted as the wife of Gilles, and I very much value my privacy. Besides, I have a very strong dislike of anyone knowing how to get in touch with me," announced a sharp, carefully cultured feminine voice that Abby had not heard in years.

But one she knew all too well.

She turned to the doorway of the room and gaped at the dark-haired, statuesque, intimidating woman standing there.

"*Tilda?*"

Coming Soon

Agents of the Convent
Book Six

"Spying is such sweet sorrow..."

by

Rebecca Connolly

About the Author

⸱────⟨❦⟩────⸱

Growing up, Rebecca Connolly wanted to be Elizabeth Bennett, Mary Poppins, or British royalty, so it came as a great shock when she discovered she was an American girl from the Midwest. She started making up stories when she was young, and thanks to a rampant imagination and a fairly consistent stream of hot chocolate, ice cream, and cookie dough, she's kept at it. She loves a good love story, and a good swoon, and tries to share that with her readers. She still lives in the Midwest, has two degrees in non-writing fields, and dreams of one day having a cottage of her own in her beloved British Isles.

Rebecca is a huge fan of period dramas and currently writes in the Regency era, though she refuses to rule any other time period out. You just never know where the imagination will take you, and she'll write whatever story comes to her whenever it's set! There is always a story to tell, and she wants to tell them all!

You can find out more at www.rebeccaconnolly.com.